MUSIC IN THE MOUNTAINS

MUSIC IN THE MOUNTAINS

Frontier Brides, Book 3

Colleen L. Reece

CHIVERS

British Library Cataloguing in Publication Data available

This Large Print edition published by AudioGO Ltd, Bath, 2012.
Published by arrangement with the Author

U.K. Hardcover   ISBN   97814458 2673 8
U.K. Softcover   ISBN   97814458 2674 5

Copyright © 1994 by Colleen L. Reece
Scripture quotations are taken from the King James Version of the Bible.

Printed and bound in Great Britain by
MPG Books Group Limited

MUSIC IN THE MOUNTAINS

PROLOGUE

*Summer 1889, Double J Ranch
near Flagstaff, Arizona*

Gideon Carroll Scott slid painfully from the saddle of his sorrel mare, Miss Bess, and dropped the reins so his well-trained horse would stand. How many times in the past thirteen years had he brought knotty problems to the rise overlooking the Double J? No matter how troubled he felt, the panoramic view never failed to restore his peace: the valley, dotted with his and Judith's cattle; cedar, pine, and a lazy stream; quaking aspens whispering secrets; distant red rimrock telling nothing.

The spread was his by the grace of God and backing from a down-on-his-luck prospector Gideon once grubstaked. His partner, Tomkins, would gleefully recount to anyone who would listen how he struck it rich, purchased most of a Colorado town that later boomed, then sold out his holdings, and with Gideon purchased the now-prosperous Arizona ranch.

Gideon limped to the edge of the rise, aware as always of the twinges from a long-ago gunshot wound. The doctor had warned him too much riding would bring pain, but the blue-eyed man whose sun-streaked hair held silver threads felt glad to be alive. A quarter-inch closer, and the bullet would have severed his spine. He shivered in the warm air. God had been good.

He looked down again. From this same point, he had seen the billowing white canvas of the Conestoga wagon that brought his unclaimed wife, Judith, to find him, along with their beloved eight-year-old nephew, Joel.

Miss Bess whinnied and nudged his shoulder with her soft nose. He absently patted her shining mane. At thirty-seven, he still became misty at the memory of the mare's mother, which had faithfully carried him for so many wandering years.

Loyal Dainty Bess had braved sun and drought, blizzard and wind, bearing on her back a bitter outcast, unjustly accused of a brother's crime. From Texas to Colorado, Wyoming to Montana, and finally to Arizona, she had carried Gideon. Even the filly she left as her legacy could never take her place, although Miss Bess had proven herself as steadfast as her mother.

Gideon turned his back on the ranch and mounted, only to silently survey the sapphire sky. If anyone had told him all those years ago the day would come when he would wait for a stage bringing the father who drove him away, he'd have laughed in their face. A trained minister, Gideon had nonetheless worn the brand of his brother's cowardice, a brand etched on his heart by his father.

"It's all behind me," he told the tiny white cloud that scooted by. "God, only You and Judith know how much it meant when my brother Cyrus sent a note asking forgiveness and confessing his guilt. I wonder . . ." He sat so still, Miss Bess tossed her head. "Will Joel find his father someday? Or does Cyrus lie somewhere beneath the dust of the tumbleweed trail?" Longing swelled within him. Not just for the coming reunion with his father and mother whom he hadn't seen in fifteen years, but for the soul of his beloved elder brother. It had taken a long time, but with God's help, Gideon had forgiven Cyrus. Now all he wanted was to know if his older brother lived and, if so, to have him find Christ.

As he turned toward home, he was met by

his nine-year-old twins racing toward him on their ponies. Millie led, as usual, with Matt just a few paces behind. How they could ride!

"I won," Millie cried, her dark brown eyes glowing like her mother's. Her long, dark brown braid was all that distinguished her from her twin.

"Aw, you got a head start." Matt brought his dancing pony to a stop. "Dad, Mother says for you to hurry or —"

"Or you'll be late picking up Grandpa and Grandma," Millie finished. A frown marred her smooth tan forehead. "I don't see why you're going and we can't."

Matt couldn't resist the urge to crow. "Anyone almost ten like we are should know. Or didn't you listen when Mother said Dad had waited a lot more years to see them than we have?"

Millie pouted a bit and threw a disdainful look at her twin. "You're so smart. I bet you don't know why Dad really wants to go by himself." She looked mysterious.

"Neither do you. You're just mad 'cause you can't go."

With the sunny quirk that kept Millie from being obnoxious when she didn't get her own way, she grinned and admitted, "So? You want to go to Flagstaff, too." She dug her heels in her pony's sides and headed for the two-story weathered ranch house, calling over her shoulder, "Race you home!"

Matt couldn't resist her challenge. He and his pony pelted after the jean-clad figure bent low over her racing steed. "Hurry up, Dad!" he called back.

Gideon breathed easier. When his prying daughter proclaimed she knew his reasons for leaving his family behind, he felt his heart bounce. He and Judith had agreed the twins need not know how deep or bitter the chasm had been between Gideon and his parents. Their quick loyalty would color their love for their grandparents and the long-missing uncle. Gideon had never lied. He merely said there had been trouble and misunderstanding. Now that Joel had grown up and ridden back over the trails Gideon traveled many years earlier, ending up at the Circle S ranch near San Scipio, Texas, outside of El Paso, the elder Scotts decided to visit. "We might even talk them into selling the Circle S and living out here," he promised.

The twins could barely wait, but Millie disconsolately said, "I wish Joel were coming with them." She sighed. "I know he's gone to look for his father, but I miss him. He's been gone forever."

11

"Not forever," her more methodical twin put in, his dark eyes teasing. "Just a year."

"That's forever." Millie sighed clear down to her boots. "Why didn't he stay here with us?"

Clear-eyed Judith tenderly smoothed her daughter's rumpled hair back from her face. The years had been kind. No trace of white lightened her dark brown braids, still worn in a coronet. Happiness with the husband she once took highlighted her still-beautiful face. "Joel went on a mission," she explained. "People your father knew a long time ago needed to hear about Jesus."

"And Dad couldn't go, so our big brother went," Millie supplied. "Except he's really our cousin, isn't he?" She didn't wait for her mother's nod. "I still call him brother, and so does Matt."

"He's the best brother in the whole world," Matt declared. Tired of inactivity, he leaped to his feet. "C'mon, Millie, let's go see what Lonesome and Dusty and the rest of the outfit's doing." They left with a familiar whoop that boded no good for any of the hands too busy to talk with them.

Now Gideon prodded Miss Bess into a gallop as he rode into the corrals. Tossing her reins to Matt, who actually had outdistanced his sister, he advised, "Take care of her, will you?"

"Sure, Dad." Pride showed in every inch of his face, but he offered generously, "You can help me, Millie. Dad has to get cleaned up, and so do we."

"Thanks," Gideon called, then swung toward the house in a long lope. The time-silvered logs little resembled the Mexican adobe home and courtyard of his youth. How would Dad and Mother like it? A prayer of longing filled him. *Please, God, let all be well and according to Your will.* He slipped inside and upstairs, hearing Judith's gentle laugh from the kitchen mingled with Millie's higher-pitched voice. Evidently the lure of grooming Miss Bess had failed to soothe the sting of a loss to her twin. A little later, Gideon ran downstairs, soap-and-water fresh, new riding outfit pressed and impressive. "How do I look?" he demanded.

"Like a happy rancher welcoming his parents to the Double J." Judith smiled from the doorway, and he felt the thrill that never failed to come when he saw her and remembered the long months when time and circumstances had separated them.

"I am, Judith. This has been one of my dreams. Now if only . . ." He swallowed. Sadness must have no place on this special day, not even the poignant longing to know about Cyrus.

"Vaya con Dios." Judith Butler Scott lifted her face for the kiss he always bestowed even when leaving for a short time. He saw the goodness, the love, and the tears she tried to hide. For a moment, Gideon held her close to his heart, then walked slowly out and climbed into the buggy his longtime foreman Fred Aldrich had waiting. He had started on his journey to weave threads from the past into the tapestry of the present.

Lige Scott turned from the stage window to the wife who had loved him so many years. His blue eyes that often looked steel hard now resembled the soft Arizona dawn. "We're almost there." Thin, gaunt, silver of hair, and furrowed of face, still the mighty head and shoulders remained erect, unbowed by his once-blind love for his older son or his unjust accusations for the younger. Time had mellowed his heart, but true repentance for accusing Gideon of Cyrus's actions had won forgiveness from his heavenly Father. The past few years, letters had flown between Texas and Arizona. Now at the urgent prodding of the golden-haired Joel, the boy preacher who had chosen to follow in his uncle's footsteps, and of white-haired Naomi, with the snap-

14

ping blue eyes and patient spirit, only minutes remained until they reached their destination.

"Naomi, has he really forgiven me?"

The same love that strengthened her through all his headstrong years of serving the Almighty according to the gospel of Elijah Scott shone in her face. "Oh ye of little faith! Gideon and Judith's letters told you that. So did Joel when he came."

The giant pioneer's mouth worked. "I haven't deserved it."

Her work-worn hand, beautiful in its mute witness of a life lived in service to God and others, gently rested on his massive, calloused paw. "Elijah, if any of us got what we deserved, God wouldn't have sent His Son to take our punishment so we could one day live with Him."

"I know. It's just that for the first time in my life, I'm afraid." The whisper barely reached her straining ears.

"I believe Gideon has forgiven you with all his heart," she told the troubled man. His convulsive grip of her hand threatened to crush bones, but a tremendous sigh heaved from the cavern of Lige's chest, and he said no more.

The long journey drew to a close. The stage slowed at the driver's bellow, "Whoa, you miserable critters!" Lige held tight rein on his desire to leap out and find his son and helped Naomi from the conveyance. He reached strong arms to accept the trunks and bags the driver pitched down. Back turned to Naomi, his keen ears caught her cry, "Gideon!"

Lige shot a prayer toward heaven. His first look into Gideon's eyes would tell him what he must know. He felt suspended in judgment between heaven and earth. Then he turned to meet his wronged son.

The steady blue eyes that had accused him in memory for fifteen years held nothing but love.

Great tearing sobs rose within him. Lige opened both arms, heedless of staring passengers and curious bystanders. "My son, my son!" Unashamed tears poured.

"Dad, welcome home."

The next instant, Lige caught Gideon in an embrace that wordlessly said what he could not. Yet the hard muscles that encircled him confirmed what the blue eyes had spoken, forgiveness surpassed only by God's gift to the world.

Another cry from Naomi opened the closed circle. Yet even the moment she had longed for ever since her younger son rode away failed to quench her indomitable

16

spirit. "Land sakes, what's all this sniveling about? We're here, aren't we, and right glad of it."

Laughter rumbled in Lige's throat and gratefulness for the release from emotions far deeper than he had ever expected. He held Gideon away. " 'Cept for some silver in your hair, you don't look any older."

"Judith and the twins are waiting," Gideon said quietly. "Mother, Dad, thank God you've come." His voice broke, and he led them to the buggy. After helping Lige load their belongings, Gideon turned the horses toward the Double J.

Summer 1890, Colorado Springs, Colorado
Eb Sears let the white pages of a just-delivered letter drift to the carpeted floor of his living room. The stocky man's big frame shook. "Dear God, is this the answer?" He thought of the recent months when his wife, Lily, had reverted to the listless woman he and Joel Scott had found more than a year before. It was then Joel had shared his message of salvation.

A wide smile crossed the weathered face as he thought of Joel. Eb looked older than his late thirties but still vulnerable as far as Lily and her six-year-old son, now his cherished stepson, were concerned. "Still

17

hard to believe what crooked paths You took to make me listen," he told God. "First off, Gideon sends his son to tell me any time I want a job in Arizona, one's waitin'.'" He shook his thatch of coarse hair. "Good thing, too. All the time he took care of me after I got shot made me see what he preached in Tomkinsville was true."

So much had happened since Joel rode away in search of his father. Eb and Lily both accepted the Lord and found love for one another. Her first husband's parents, who kept her when he died, had met with a fatal accident, leaving Lily bereft. A few weeks earlier, she had cried out, "Eb, can't we sell the store and go away? I don't want to live here anymore."

A million prayers followed and then to-day . . . Eb reread the missive from Gideon Scott, a man he once despised.

We're still hoping you and Lily and young Danny will come to the Double J. Tomkins and I are expanding our holdings, and there's plenty of room in this wild land for us all. I've never forgotten that you could have let me hang for a crime I didn't commit. Joel sent word you and Lily had given your lives to God. Eb, you'll never regret it.

My parents have decided to sell out in Texas and stay here. The best news of all is that Joel located Cyrus, has fallen in love with his adopted daughter, Rebecca, and hopes to come west soon.

Why don't you join them? Flagstaff needs more Christian settlers and ranchers. I can't ride as long and far as I'd like. The bullet one of Zeke Stockton's men put in me saw to that. I haven't told Judith, but rumors have it Stockton didn't go straight after we released him; that he's in up to his sombrero with one of the worst bands of outlaws and rustlers in the Tonto, where he built a home.

We need you, Eb. Will you come? Of course, if Lily won't leave Colorado Springs, I'll understand.

The scrawled signature, *Gideon Scott,* sent a wave of longing through Eb. More convinced than ever that God had nudged Gideon into writing at just this time, Eb bounded into the bedroom where Lily sat looking out the window. "How would you like to go to Arizona?" he asked.

The dark-eyed, dark-haired child who sat leaning against her rocker leaped to his feet. "Daddy, Daddy, can I have a pony?"

"I wouldn't be surprised." Eb caught

19

Danny up and hugged him. He couldn't love the boy more if Danny were his own. "Well, Lily?"

A faint color stained her thin white cheeks. With an obvious effort, she stood and ran to him. "I'm ready to leave tomorrow." The strength of her arms surprised him.

"Whoa, there," Eb told them when Danny squealed and clapped his hands. "First we have to sell the store and house, then get outfitted. Gideon suggests we travel by way of Texas and meet up with Joel."

Lily stiffened in his arms. He glanced at her in dismay and said, "Run along, Buckaroo. Your mother and I have some talkin' to do."

"We're going to Arizona, we're going to Arizona," Danny chanted into her face.

"Is somethin' wrong?" He held her out from him and peered anxiously into her face.

Dread had replaced her eagerness, and she drooped in his arms. Past thirty, to her husband she looked no older than she had at seventeen, although thinner and more worn. "Eb, will I be welcome?" A slight red crept into her cheeks, and her dark eyes misted.

"Welcome! I should smile." He stared at her, unable to believe his ears. "Why, just read this." He spread the pages before her and pointed out the places where Gideon so warmly encouraged them to come. "Why should you — ?"

Her head rested on his broad chest. How easily she tired. "They all know I sang in the Missing Spur."

Understanding filled him, and his arms tightened. "You were an innocent kid who had to eat, and you did nothin' ever to be ashamed of," he told her fiercely. "Think Gideon would have staked you and got you away if he hadn't known you were just plain good all the way through?" He picked her up, crossed to the rocker, and cradled her as if she were a baby. " 'Sides, even if you hadn't been good — and you were — remember what Joel said? Jesus ain't carin' about the past. Once we give Him us, why, that's all that matters." He stilled the rocker. "Lily, Girl, if God kept count of all our sins, we'd all be goners, 'specially me."

She burst into healing tears, the first that had fallen since the double funeral. "It's just that I want you and Danny to be proud of me. Gideon married a real lady, and I'll bet Joel will, too."

The big man who found it hard to open his heart took a deep breath, then slowly released it. "I loved you from the minute I saw you. Nothin' ever changed that. Nothin' ever will. You know Gideon and Joel. Reckon they'd ever get hitched to anyone not just as lovin' and carin'?"

"N-no." She nestled closer in his arms.

Danny burst back in, putting an end to confidences. When he ran to them, trouble sponged all the joy from his face. "Mama, you're crying. Don't you want to go to Arizona?" With an obvious effort, he swallowed and said, "We c'n stay here; just don't cry."

He looked so forlorn standing there that Eb shifted Lily and put Danny on his knee. "Son, Mama's crying 'cause she's happy. We'll go to Arizona as soon as we sell our holdin's."

"God'll help us," Danny confidently told them. He slid down and trotted to the door. "Better get packed. God does things real fast!"

The young boy's prophecy came true. In less than a week, the Searses had buyers for both store and house. They joyously thanked their heavenly Father and rejoiced that the good prices would allow them to purchase land in Arizona. Recent telegrams convinced them not to go by way of Texas. Since Joel's ever-growing caravan now planned to go by Conestoga wagon, Lily's frail constitution would be pushed to the utmost.

Instead, Eb purchased passage by stage. They would travel straight through to Arizona and be there long before Joel's wagon train arrived. The little family knelt together and asked God's help for a safe journey. As they walked away from the house that had never really felt like home, Danny expressed their feelings aptly. " 'Bye, house. We won't never see you no more 'cause we're off to Arizona." He tugged at Eb's sleeves. "Don't forget my pony."

Eb, who had never been out of Colorado, looked down at the child. "I won't, Son." His gaze met Lily's, and a slow smile crept to his lips. "It won't be long 'fore we're all fat and sassy." He knew his laughing words conveyed what his grateful heart could not.

CHAPTER 1

Summer 1890, Circle S Ranch,
San Scipio, Texas

"Hey, Boss, what's eatin' Smokey?" Bow-legged Jim Perkins shoved his sweat-stained Stetson far back on his head and cocked an eyebrow. Joel Scott tore his blue gaze from the stubborn canvas he'd finally secured over the hoops of the Conestoga wagon. This hospital on wheels would soon make the long journey to Flagstaff, Arizona, and his uncle Gideon's Double J ranch. His tousled golden hair formed a skewed halo around his rugged, tanned face, which could look younger than twenty and older than the steeply sloping mesa above the Circle S. "Is something eating him?"

"Is somethin' eatin' him!" Jim, just a few years older than his new boss, rolled his eyes toward heaven. "Snappin' crocodiles, if yu ain't deaf, dumb, and blind!" He removed his hat, slapped it against his dusty jeans,

25

and crammed it back on his head. "Haw, haw, bein' in love's made yu plumb loco." When a wave of red swept into Joel's face, the clear-eyed, lovable cowboy went on.

"Now some folks can handle love and dooty all at the same time. Take me, f'r instance. Do I let my purty little wife, Conchita, keep me from my chores? Umpumm." The teasing gave way to a warm glance. "Have to admit, it makes comin' home and findin' her waitin' real good." With his lightning ability to change moods, he added, "When're yu and Rebecca gettin' hitched?"

Joel completed his struggle with the billowing white top that gave covered wagons the nickname *prairie schooners.* The same glow he'd seen in Jim's eyes brightened his own into twin lakes. "We decided to wait until we get to the Double J. Samuel, I mean, Cyrus said he knew the folks would be pleased."

"I don't know. Our little jaunt woulda made an awful nice honeymoon." Jim grinned. "Come to think of it, that's just what Connie 'n' me will have."

Now came Joel's turn to tease. Although his faith in God and ability to clearly present his Master's message of hope and salvation had earned him the title of boy preacher, he could hold his own with his sometimes cantankerous, always alert companions. "Of course you won't want to let sparking interfere with your dooties." He carefully mimicked Jim's pronunciation.

"No more than your spoonin' under the New Mexico and Arizona stars," Jim shot back. "Now gettin' back to Smokey —"

"I honestly haven't noticed a thing," Joel confessed. His strong hands stilled. "Everything's happened so fast since the showdown with Hayes. Finding out Samuel Fairfax is really my father, Cyrus, and no kin to Rebecca; getting him fit enough to bring back here from the Lazy F; selling the ranch and all the horses and cattle except what we're driving to Arizona. . . ." He paused, looking troubled. "You don't think Smokey's regretting leaving New Mexico, do you? He could have stayed on the Lazy F as foreman. Lundeen of the Bar Triangle was glad to expand and all but begged Smokey to stay."

"Naw, that ain't it a-tall," Jim disagreed. A wise look crept into his far-seeing eyes. "I kinda got a hunch, and if it's what I think, he'll get worse or better." He grinned tormentingly at his boss, sauntered off, and left Joel with the urge to throttle him.

"He and Smokey are no different from

27

Lonesome and Dusty back home," he muttered. A thrill of anticipation assaulted him. If all went well, the caravan would start their drive to the Double J in just a few days. He forgot all about Smokey Travis's possible problems in the excitement and need to remember a hundred details.

Inside the sprawling adobe home, Cyrus Scott gazed about with mingled emotions. The thick walls, impervious to heat and cold, had housed him for twenty-four careless years. *If only I could relive them,* he thought desperately. Not only those first years of his life but many more had been wasted because of his rebellious desire to ride the range, take what he wanted, and let the other fellow be hanged. In the time since he'd been shot, Cyrus had had ample time to consider the results of his actions. If he hadn't secretly married Millicent Butler, using his younger brother's name, he wouldn't be lying here filled with dread at meeting Gideon again after sixteen long, empty years. Although Joel repeatedly had assured him he'd been forgiven years before, Cyrus still had his doubts.

Joel. A smile of pride crept over the tired face as gratitude filled him. Had any man ever had such a son? He scoffed at the idea.

How many young men would take up a work begun by another, travel back over untamed trails, and right wrongs with the sword of truth?

"Father?" A soft voice interrupted his musings, and he turned his graying head. Rebecca, the girl entrusted to his care and whom he loved more than any daughter, stood near. Her merry brown eyes sparkled, and an errant ray of sun through the window gilded her nut-brown hair. Soon she would be his daughter by law. What a pair she and Joel would make! They were both dedicated to the Lord Cyrus had only begun to know personally, although he'd been taught about God and Jesus since the cradle.

"You should see the wagon!" She clapped her hands, and a rich smile curved her lips. "The bed must be ten feet long and a good four feet wide. We'll put in feather ticks, and you can ride on top of them comfortable as a king." Her laugh rang like a string of silver bells on a horse's harness. "Joel just got the canvas on — it's been water-proofed for days — and the sides slide up so you can have fresh air and see out." She stepped closer, and he saw the little gold sparkles that danced in her eyes when she got excited. "You really are well enough, aren't you? We don't have to go yet."

"Well enough!" Rotund Mrs. Cook, fresh-faced and motherly, marched into the room. "If he gets any better, I won't be able to keep him from mounting a horse and setting off alone." With the familiarity of years as Cyrus and Rebecca's cook and housekeeper, she frankly stated her opinion whenever it suited her.

"I'm so glad you're going with us!" Rebecca hugged her friend and adviser.

"And where else would I be if I didn't? Think I'd let you two head off to Arizona and leave me behind to miss all the fun?" Her hands worked as she talked, twitching the sheets and pillows, smoothing the light blanket over her employer's feet.

"Let's see." Rebecca ticked off on her fingers. "There'll be we three; Joel, Jim, and Conchita, that's six. Curly, who straight out and said he'd be glad to 'mosey along' and help with the cookin'. I wasn't sure he'd leave the Bar Triangle and Lundeen." Her eyes filled with mischief. "I think he figures he'd be lonesome without Mrs. Cook."

Cyrus laughed, but the worthy woman's mouth turned down, although a twinkle in her eyes belied her true feelings. "More'n likely he's trying to show folks he's a better cook than I am. Well, we'll see. I never did cook for the hands, as you well remember,

30

and I don't intend to start now. Let Curly feed them."

"But we're the hands," Rebecca laughingly protested. "Think I'm going to ride in the wagon with Father? Vermilion's just hankering for the chance to help drive the herd, and so am I. Smokey said . . ." She broke off. "Have either of you noticed how quiet Smokey is lately?"

Mrs. Cook snorted. "As if a body didn't have enough to do with packing and planning. You do run on, Child." She started for the door. "If you think something's wrong, why don't you just up and ask him?" She went out and closed the door behind her.

"Well?" Cyrus looked at his daughter who glanced down at the cook's parting shot.

"I don't think I can." Confusion showed in her blooming face, and she bit her lip. "Smokey's too bighearted to have bad feelings toward Joel, yet once he cared for me. I always felt toward him like a sister."

Cyrus warmed to her confidences. In all the years he'd lived under a cloud, she hadn't been able to get through his bull-headed determination to run her life. He couldn't remember a time when she'd talked with him as she did now. "Rebecca, I wouldn't worry too much about Travis. Right now, he's probably doing a lot of thinking, maybe just adjusting his feelings toward you. I'm sure Smokey never felt he had a chance. He was simply your good friend when you needed one badly. Once we get to Arizona, why, he'll meet a girl and fall in love with her. He loves Joel like a brother, and not just because Joel saved his life. Don't fret about it. Just be the same friend you've always been."

"Thank you, Father." She stooped and kissed him, and Cyrus felt a drop fall to his cheek. With light steps, she crossed the room. "Rest as much as you can. It's a long way to Arizona."

And to Gideon and Dad, he mentally added.

In spite of the increasing last-moment preparations, Joel managed to keep an eye out for his pard Smokey. He saw nothing amiss and wrote off Perkins's croakings as a wild imagination. Rebecca said nothing more as she was caught up with household duties, along with the others.

Handsome, dark-eyed, dark-haired Smokey Travis faithfully performed every job given to him. A top hand, he had stayed on the Lazy F for three years, far longer than most of the cowpunchers who'd been driven away by the merciless Hayes, usually for daring to be pleasant to Rebecca. Time and again, the good-natured Smokey with his droll sense of humor swallowed Hayes's goading or blunted it with a grin. His keen eyes saw danger in Cyrus's association with a foreman he obviously disliked but kept on.

"Doggone it, something's gnawing on me," he admitted one afternoon. Chores done, Jim had sought Conchita, and Joel and Rebecca had drifted off together. Even Curly had deserted and dared approach Mrs. Cook in the kitchen. Smokey heard them wrangling and grinned. Then the smile faded from his pleasant lips. He headed for the corral and talked to the horses. Vermilion, the red mustang he'd caught and tamed for Rebecca's eighteenth birthday the previous December, nickered and raced toward him. The buckskin Smokey usually rode followed.

"How about you, Kay-reeda?" Smokey called to the shining black mare that had carried Joel on the long trek from Arizona.

Querida tossed her mane and edged closer. Beloved by name, beloved by her owner, she and Vermilion offered a sight that made the horse-loving cowboy's eyes glisten. "Someday we'll put you in a real race," he promised. His lean face glowed at the prospect. "That other time was no contest." Memories of the desperate race to catch the crooked Hayes galloped through his mind, a race that ended in tragedy for the thieving foreman, but in freedom for Rebecca and her father.

The red stallion turned and nudged Querida, who whinnied softly. Thunder-struck, Smokey slapped his knee. "Well, I'll be! That's it." Relief spilled into laughter. "I'll be switched if I don't have a case of the two by twos."

The buckskin nuzzled his shoulder, and he talked to her the way he'd done many times during lonely night watches. "You know that ark Joel talks about. Two by two, that's how they came. An' that's how it's getting around here." His laughter died as suddenly as it had come. When had glad-ness for his pards become tarnished with a longing to possess what they did? Smokey forgot the Circle S and the upcoming trip and daydreamed against the fence. Someday he'd like to have a spread of his own, a little place where he could bring a girl as sweet and charming and good as Conchita or Re-becca. "Never was good enough for Becky," he muttered, his gaze toward the west and new beginnings. "Joel's just what she needs, an' am I ever glad he came lookin' for his daddy. I wonder . . ." The patient buckskin never learned what it was her rider wondered. A hail from the house cut into Smokey's soliloquy, and with a final pat, he headed where duty called.

Yet once the idea had been planted, Smokey began to look forward to Arizona. He only grinned when Perkins solemnly told him Arizona girls were said to be fighting wildcats. "I've wrangled with wildcats before," he loftily told Jim. "The secret to it's all in knowing how to handle them an' never letting them get the best of you."

His loyal, heckling friend shook his head disbelievingly. "Aw, you ain't never even seen the kind of wildcats that live in Arizona." To prove his point, that night when everyone gathered for supper, he innocently asked Joel, "What's it really like where yu come from? Now that it's gonna be our home, mebbe we'd better know what to expect."

Joel leaned back in his chair, eyes half closed. "It's different from Utah or Colorado, New Mexico or Texas. There's a kind of music in the Arizona mountains and canyons."

"Music?" Rebecca's eyes looked like big brown saucers. "You mean singing?"

"That's only part of it," he eagerly told her and the others. "Although more and

35

more God-fearing families are coming to add their voices to the good old hymns. Arizona's music is more than that. It's bawling cattle and whispering aspens. It's thunder, lightning, rain, hail. Shouting riders and quiet nights. The rattle of a snake giving a warning or the snarl of an angry bobcat or mountain lion. The growl of a bear protecting her cubs, the sound of snow falling from a cabin roof or tree branch." Sadness shadowed his youthful face. "It's the sound of rifles and Colts in the hands of those who prey, those who defy them; the sizzle of a red-hot branding iron, the scream of an eagle or wild horse." His gaze rested on Rebecca's brown head. "It's the croon of a mother tending a sick child, the sound of children laughing in a meadow of blowing flowers, the rumble and roar of floodwaters pounding through the echoing canyon. It's also a whisper in the wilderness, the voice of God pleading with hearts to receive Him."

Smokey silently stood and slipped out. Why should his eyes sting and the very soul within him cry out to be part of the music in the mountains? His stomach felt hollow and empty, although supper had been ample and he'd eaten prodigiously. From force of habit, he turned toward the corral, cut out the buckskin, and rode into the summer night. Plenty of music here, too, if a man considered the chirp of crickets and crying nightbirds' music. Straight to the promontory that overlooked the Circle S he rode, never knowing that first Gideon, then Judith, and later Joel had sought out the same spot.

Under the Texas sky, Smokey Travis realized the longing within him had a deeper meaning than he had thought. While he still clung to his dream of a wife and someday kids of his own, he had been stirred to the depths of his being by Joel's words and the reverence in his voice.

He drew a long, quivering breath. He could still see the look on his friend's face, the radiance and the shining goodness mingled with humility.

"That Trailmate of his must make him like that," Smokey pondered. "Wonder if a plain old cowpuncher like me could ever get that way?" He shrugged off the idea. Life on the frontier trying to survive, homeless, without folks, hadn't been easy. He had seen the worst and the best, falling somewhere between them. Skilled with horse, rope, Colt, and rifle, something had held him back from following the downward path that ended in debauchery. He'd seen too many who took it. Smokey had also avoided women; that is, until he met Rebecca Fairfax. He had been glad he could look her square in the eye without stains on his soul. He still was. No matter what the future held, her girlish innocence had fostered in the trailhand the knowledge that unless he found another as clean and high-spirited, he must ride alone.

At last they were ready. On Saturday, the eight who would share the hardships and joys of the trail gathered in the partially dismantled home. Many precious belongings must remain, but Cyrus had selected the choicest of the blankets, pictures and hangings, and the carved candlesticks and other special items his mother cherished. Already they lay packed into a second wagon, where Rebecca and Mrs. Cook would sleep. Curly had surprised them by claiming experience and insisting he would drive one of the wagons. Mrs. Cook looked at him suspiciously, but his usual jolly manner hid any devious scheme he might be concocting. Jim and Conchita had a small "honeymoon wagon," and he, Joel, and Smokey would take turns driving it while the others managed the herd. At the last minute, a surprisingly generous offer from the Circle S buyer had further depleted the cattle. The two men with the help of an insistent Rebecca and Conchita could handle them, with Curly helping stand night guard.

"I think it is fitting that we rest on the Sabbath and begin our journey the next day," Cyrus told them. "Besides, I'd like to hear Joel preach."

A slow color spread over the young minister's face, but his blue gaze never wavered. "I'd be happy to preach," he told them simply.

The next day, they met in a shady grove that offered protection against the scorching sun. Dressed in clean but plain clothing, they sang the beloved old hymns Joel had said were part of the music of Arizona. Now that the time had come, there was no looking back. Ahead lay adventure, challenge, life.

And love? Smokey wondered. *Will Arizona fill the hole inside me?* Would its wind and storm and battering rain that brought years-old seed alive and blooming until the desert lay carpeted with flowers satisfy his inner restlessness? He thought of the red-rock canyons Joel described. Of the icy, rushing streams; the snowcapped mountains; the Mogollon [muh-gee-yohn] Rim and Tonto Basin, wild as the day they were created and filled with dark, silent men who kept apart from those not of their own. Surely somewhere he would find what he sought.

Smokey jerked his attention back to Joel, whose face glowed with an inner light. Still caught up in his daydreams, the cowboy let his tanned hands gently rest on his knees. He heard Joel say he would read from 1 Kings 19:11-12. The next moment, the words snatched Smokey's full attention.

And he said, Go forth, and stand upon the mount before the Lord. And, behold, the Lord passed by, and a great and strong wind rent the mountains, and brake in pieces the rocks before the Lord; but the Lord was not in the wind: and after the wind an earthquake; but the Lord was not in the earthquake:

And after the earthquake a fire; but the Lord was not in the fire: and after the fire a still small voice."

Joel paused. Smokey stared at him with unseeing eyes. How many times had he stood on mountains and felt the ground slide beneath his feet, not from earthquakes but from loose shale. The sensation of having the earth on which he stood quivering, breaking free, brought terror. How many

40

windstorms had he breasted, exultant, glorying in the gale that wreaked havoc in forests and shrieked across the land! He had seen fire in all its mad beauty, devouring the prairie, greedily taking the grass that cattle and horses and deer needed to survive. And the lightning strikes that toppled and turned giant trees to ugly black snags, reminders of the forces of unleashed nature.

Smokey marveled, recalling certain phrases from the Scripture reading. *The Lord was not in the wind . . . not in the earthquake . . . not in the fire . . . after . . . a still small voice.* His heart and mind rebelled. The God he knew was in all those things. Although he'd not put it into words, Smokey felt no one could witness the things he had seen and not know Someone stood behind them.

He didn't hear the rest of Joel's sermon. If all his years of finding the Creator in dust and wind, cyclone and blizzard, thunder and lightning meant nothing . . . He struggled to understand. Why would a God so great He could inspire followers to become His messengers, as Joel Scott had done, whisper in a still small voice? Wouldn't He shout from the tallest peak, proclaim His majesty in a booming voice magnified by canyon walls?

Strangely disappointed, Smokey left the service feeling emptier than ever.

CHAPTER 2

"Rebecca, are you sure you don't want to change your mind about going with the herd?" Joel anxiously surveyed his fiancée, whose tumbled brown curls formed a halo around her laughing face. "The Southern Pacific will get you and Cyrus to Arizona a whole lot faster than our wagon train."

She looked surprised. "We settled that a long time ago. Father will be fine, and I wouldn't miss this trip for all the trains in the West. Soon wagon travel will be a thing of the past. I want to be able to tell our children their parents once pioneered, just as their grandparents did." A lovely color came into her face.

"That's what I wanted to hear," Joel admitted. After glancing both ways to make sure the cottonwood grove was deserted, he passionately took Rebecca in his arms. "If I live to be a hundred, I'll never stop thanking God for leading me to you — and to

Dad," he said softly as he rested his chin on top of her shining head.

"Only a hundred? Piker!"

He tilted her head back with one forefinger and kissed her. Rebecca's arms stole up and around his neck, and for a long, precious moment, they stood together, welded by love and hope for the future.

A dozen yards away, Smokey turned from the charming scene. A familiar pang went through him. Would he ever get used to seeing Joel and Rebecca or Jim and Conchita kissing without wishing for a girl of his own?

Don't be a fool, he told himself. *You aren't an old man at twenty-one. There's plenty of time, an' remember what Jim said about Arizona girls.* He stifled a laugh and was about to sneak off, unwilling to be caught spying on his boss and friend, but then he stopped in his tracks. "Not my fault if every time I turn around, I fall over them, is it?" he demanded of the empty sky. Smokey snorted, called himself a fool again, and went back to the last-minute jobs. They'd be leaving within an hour. Gladness filled him, and his dark eyes sparkled. Would Arizona prove to be as grand and wild as Joel described?

"It'll have to go some to beat New Mexico," the lithe rider decided aloud.

"Leastways, the parts I've ridden." He thought of the fan-shaped scene visible from the Lazy F: forested slopes, rolling plains, the old Santa Fe Trail, the Cimarron River. Thousands of acres with only a few cattle ranches, spreading west like a lava flow past slopes that rose into jutting snowcapped peaks. "Kit Carson, Maxwell, and other old-timers were right," he mused. "They called it the grandest sight in New Mexico. Maybe I should have taken Lundeen up on his offer. Foreman of the Lazy F, pretty fine-sounding. Wonder if it's too late? I helped Joel get his daddy home to Texas. I could go back."

He shook his dark head, and a poignant light crept into his dark eyes. Joel Scott and Jim Perkins were the best pards he'd ever had. He'd trail along to Arizona with them. If he didn't like it, he could move on. "Anyway, I guess I have to learn more about that Trailmate of the boss's," he muttered half under his breath.

"What're yu mumblin' about?" Perkins, whose face looked mischievous all the time and downright devilish most of the time, grinned and raised one eyebrow.

"Just thinking. Mostly about how some fellers get to drive a wagon with a pretty little filly next to them an' other poor

45

cowpokes are left to eat dust and nurse bad-tempered critters," Smokey shot back.

"Hey, Pard, yu c'n drive Connie part of the time if yu like, if yu promise not to tell her ever'thin' yu know about me." Jim grinned again.

"Huh, why would I want to ride with an old married woman, even one as good-looking as Conchita?" Smokey glared at his bosom buddy. Some impulse made him add, "You just wait 'til we roll into Arizona. Why, I'll bet Joel's uncle Gideon's told all the gals from Flag to Phoenix I'm coming." Smokey closed his eyes and let his face relax into a smile. "I can see it now. A great big parade with girls in fluffy dresses an' a band; there's probably a banner saying, 'Here comes Smokey Travis, the best dog-gone cowpuncher in Texas, New Mexico, an' all of Arizona.' " He opened his eyes.

"Yu con-ceited rooster," Jim told him disgustedly. "Yu'll be lucky if one girl's there, let alone a whole herd of 'em." His face brightened. " 'Course, if she's like Connie or Becky, yu only need one." He pounded his sparring partner on the back until Smokey told him to lay off, they had work to do.

One of the decisions Joel had made about the trip was for each of them to have an

46

equal voice in all decisions. They had spent hours poring over maps. Cyrus proved invaluable in their plans because of his earlier wanderings. He didn't know Arizona, but he'd ridden through much of New Mexico. Joel remembered a surprising amount from when he and Judith crossed with Tomkins, even though he'd been young. Smokey, Jim, and Curly added their two cents.

"The way I see it," Smokey said in one of their sessions, "it's roughly 450 miles from the Circle S to Phoenix; after that, there's another 150 on to Flagstaff and the Double J. That's 600 miles. Now allowing for heat an' dust an' cranky cows, we'll do good if we make 15 to 20 miles a day."

"Yu mean I got thirty or forty days to sit next to Connie?" Jim gleefully asked, and his handsome wife blushed like a late summer rose.

"Yeah, an' thirty or forty nights to take turns singing to the herd," Smokey reminded.

Jim's chagrin was painted all over his weathered face. "Aw, I never thought of that."

Rebecca spoke up, her eyes like brown stars. "I thought the early pioneers always made at least twenty miles a day."

"Ump-umm," Curly disagreed, his jolly face set in concentration. "The pioneers usually had oxen or mules. We're using horses."

"Father, why didn't the earlier pioneers use horses?" Rebecca wanted to know.

Cyrus looked thoughtful. "They needed to carry more grain with them. Mules were unsuitable because they ate the bark from cottonwoods, hated heavy loads, and, of course, had bad dispositions. Oxen, on the other hand, could pull more and get along on prairie grass."

"Are we going to carry enough grain for our animals in case we don't find grass?" she asked doubtfully. "We're taking an awful lot of other things."

"You should see the way we're going to pack," Joel reassured her.

Mrs. Cook eyed him distrustfully and demanded, "You aren't filling up the wagons so much I can't ride, are you? I'm not walking to Arizona, and that's final." She tossed her silver-touched brown head indignantly, and her blue eyes flashed.

"No one's walking. Rebecca's already decided to ride Vermilion most of the way. Conchita can walk or ride as she chooses. Cyrus gets the feather bed 'hospital wagon,' and the rest of us will ride and trade off driving," Joel reassured.

Rebecca giggled. "If this were a few years ago, we'd never dare start off with just three wagons for fear of Indians. I'm glad it's 1890 and there's no more fighting."

"Just 'cause Geronimo surrendered four years ago and stopped the Apache raids on lonely outposts an' ranches, even on forts an' towns, doesn't mean that all Arizona Territory's troubles are over," Smokey somberly pointed out. "According to Joel here, his old stomping grounds have got their share of rustlers and outlaws like Hayes."

"That's right. Stockton, whom the Double J boys drove out of the Flag area, has set up business in the Tonto, one of the wildest areas in the whole territory. Gideon says nothing's been proved, but if range gossip is to be believed, Stockton hasn't mended either the fences he tore down or his ways." A frown wrinkled his forehead.

Smokey lounged against the back of his chair. "Men like Hayes an' this Stockton don't last long. By the time we get to the Double J, he may be six feet under." His eyes glittered. "If not, I'll have to have a little confab with him."

"Why yu?" Perkins leaped up, eyes flashing. "Since when d'yu kill the snakes for the whole outfit?"

Friendship warmed in Smokey's voice. "The way I figure, you an' Joel, maybe even Curly by the time we get to Arizona, have womenfolk to tend to." He ignored Mrs. Cook's protest and the red that seeped into Curly's round face. "Now I'm just a free an' riding cowboy whose job is to convince those snakes to rattle elsewhere." A steely glint in his dark eyes showed that beneath the raillery, he meant every word.

"Mercy, let's not be killing rattlesnakes before we ever leave Texas," Rebecca protested, and the tension lessened. But Joel followed Smokey outside with Jim at their heels.

"Killing isn't the way to go," he told them. "Only God has the power of life and death."

"With all due respect, Boss, tell that to Stockton," Perkins said. His face set into hard lines and changed from its usual cast until he looked years older and more range-wise. "A man's gotta perfect his women-folk."

The stubborn expression on Joel's face showed clearly the matter was not closed.

Bright and beautiful, departure day came. Smokey mounted the horse he'd never called anything except Buckskin, insisting a horse should be given a name that made sense. A little apart, he watched the colorful scene that spread in front of the ranch house. What a picture Rebecca made, mounted on Vermilion, her cheeks redder than his gleaming hide. Tall and golden-haired, Joel sat in Querida's saddle as if he'd been born there. The black impatiently tossed her magnificent body. Again Smokey vowed that one day they must race.

He turned toward Rosa and Carmelita, the tearful servants who had chosen to remain on the Circle S and be near their families, then to the three white-topped wagons. Jim Perkins waved his hat and hollered. Beaming Conchita clung to his arm. Curly sat straight and proud next to Mrs. Cook, her gaze straight toward the west. Smokey grinned. If he knew his onions — and he did — by the time they reached the Double J, there might just be two weddings coming off. He'd seen a fond look in the cook's eyes, and in spite of her protesting, Mrs. Cook wasn't totally immune to Curly's good nature and obliging willingness.

The most amazing facet of the entire caravan was the third wagon driver. Smokey marveled at how fast Cyrus Scott's wound had healed once they reached the Circle S. The cowboy narrowed his eyes as he realized that now, perhaps for the first time in his life, Cyrus had something to live for. If Jim and Curly looked proud, the prodigal son wore pure triumph that dropped years from his visage. Head high, hands strong on the reins, he controlled the horses with a cluck and gentle touch that would grow firm when needed.

Earlier, Smokey had overheard a conversation between Joel and his father. "You're not going to drive, Dad. It's a hospital wagon, a place you can rest. We have a long journey ahead and —"

"And I'm smart enough to know when I've had enough," Cyrus reminded his stripling son with some of the imperiousness that he had shown toward the hands as Samuel Fairfax.

"Promise you'll cry quits when you start feeling tired?" Blue gaze met blue gaze, and Smokey held his breath. He let it out in a sigh of relief when Cyrus flung an arm over his son's shoulders.

"Do you think I'll take any chances on not reaching my father — and Gideon?"

Effectively silenced, Joel said no more, and Smokey stole away. The change in the employer who had once fired him off the Lazy F was even more startling than his physical recovery. Smokey knew it would give him food for thought on the long trip west.

"At least we ain't herdin' no milk cows," Perkins sang out.

Smokey shuddered. Along with the other cowboys, he recognized the need for dairy cattle but secretly held in his contempt. The only true cow critter belonged to the range.

Joel's clear voice broke the hush that had descended. "Father, be with us. Not just for this journey but always. In the name of Your Son, who came to save us. Amen."

Smokey blinked. How could such a small prayer leave him feeling grateful and at peace with all the hardships they might have to face before they reached the Double J?

Joel raised his hand to give the signal for starting, but a swiftly moving horse heading toward them stilled his motion. "Who on earth — ?"

Like statues in a park, the little band froze. Anyone riding like that meant business. Dread settled its blanket over the travelers. Bad news came on racing horses too many times.

As the horse reached them, the thin rider straightened. "Mrs. Baker? Lucinda?" Joel finally asked the panting figure.

Lucinda Baker slid from the saddle and leaned against her heavily breathing horse for support. Her straw-colored hair had escaped its moorings and straggled from under her riding hat. Yet the gray eyes held light and determination. "I heard you were leaving." She marched unerringly toward the wagon where Cyrus Scott sat with a puzzled expression.

"A year ago, I confessed my sins to your son, how all the time I knew the way you had ridden," Lucinda said. "Cyrus, will you forgive me?" She held out a shaking hand. "God has, and I'll never get to Arizona to ask Gideon's forgiveness. Will you give it in my stead?"

Smokey saw the struggle in Cyrus Scott's face, the distaste at being reminded of a painful time long ago. The next moment, pity welled into the blue eyes so like his son's. "I will." He took her hand and said softly, "I'll tell Gideon."

Lucinda's gray eyes softened, and her shoulders squared. "Thank you." She turned to go.

"Wait," Joel told her. "Please go inside and have something cool to drink before you ride back to San Scipio."

Their last picture of home as they pulled over the first hill was of three women, Lucinda's tall figure flanked by the weeping Rosa and Carmelita, their white handkerchiefs waving in the wind.

"That took guts," Perkins murmured to Smokey when he rode alongside the wagon for a minute.

The mounted cowboy tucked the incident away in his knapsack of things to consider later.

A merry-spirited crew gathered around for a bounteous repast Mrs. Cook and the young women prepared for supper that night. "Driving a wagon and taking turns standing night guard are enough," Mrs. Cook ordered Curly in front of everyone. "No cooking for you on this jaunt."

"Yes, Ma'am," he meekly answered, but the secretive glance he shot toward Smokey from under his lowered sombrero was anything but meek. The cowboy grinned in return. Good old Curly had completely succumbed to the buxom housekeeper's charms but was wise enough not to show it. Later that evening, when he relieved Smokey, who had volunteered for first watch, his friend confirmed it.

"No use scaring the bird you want to catch," Curly smugly said, and Smokey laughed until his sides hurt.

"This here trip's just one thing after another," Smokey told Buckskin another scorching afternoon. "We haven't had to ford any rivers 'cause they don't have water in them, leastways, not more than a trickle or two. On the other hand, since there's no rain to fill the rivers, green grass there isn't." After that complicated sentence, which made perfect sense to Smokey and probably to his horse, he took off his Stetson, mopped sweat from his forehead, and jammed the hat back on.

The relentless summer sun succeeded in sapping the energy of the once-sturdy travelers. A unanimous vote by the group created the following travel plan: Begin traveling as soon after the first light as possible, and go until it got unbearably hot; if any shade offered itself, stop, rest through the burning afternoons, and go on in early evening. The first day on the new schedule, they realized the folly of continuing once the sun plopped behind the horizon. Trying to care for the stock in the almost-instant darkness proved to be too much of a burden.

Smokey sometimes wondered at the absence of complaining, even in the worst conditions. The day they got caught by a dust storm while miles from any kind of shelter, no one bellyached. They just sat it out, crawled from beneath the covering of whitish gray, did the best they could with a limited amount of water, and hoped for a better day tomorrow.

True to his inner predictions and the entire company's amusement, genial Curly's attentions to Mrs. Cook slowly began to bear fruit. From grudging tolerance to appreciation of his invariable good nature, the motherly woman continued to scold, but genuine regard appeared in her eyes. It changed to frank caring, unashamed and declared, the day she went for water at the rock-rimmed pool that apparently never went dry. Intent on getting her bucket filled, she failed to see the sidewinder coiled on the rocks. Its warning rattle came so close to its strike, she had no time to escape.

She dropped the bucket and cried out. Curly reached her first, in a burst of speed that seemed incredible due to his size. She held out her hand, marred by the tiny dots. "It bit me."

Quick as a heartbeat, Curly sprang for the cooking fire. He snatched a knife and ran back to Mrs. Cook, then grabbed her hand and slashed across the bitten area and the cut. The knife clattered to the ground. Curly jerked the cut hand to his lips, placed his mouth over the bleeding area, and sucked and spat. Again. And again, while his patient stood rigid. He only stopped long enough to gasp, "Bind her arm," then sucked and spat again.

Smokey ripped his neckerchief off and wound it above the wrist. He knotted it snugly enough to prevent the poison from spreading up Mrs. Cook's arm but loosely enough to slip his finger under it and release the pressure for a short time every ten minutes. Perkins ran for soap and water, hot as Mrs. Cook could tolerate. When Curly finally stopped his treatment, Jim quickly washed the wound, and Smokey bandaged it lightly.

"I'm all right," Mrs. Cook protested, but her voice shook. "Is Curly — ?" A sob completed her question.

"I'm fine, Ma'am, and you will be, too." Curly turned toward Joel. " 'Twouldn't hurt none for you to make a prayer."

Thanks to the older hand's quick action and the faith of those around her, Mrs. Cook suffered far less than could be expected. When some swelling developed and she felt weak, they made camp for an extra day. By the second morning, she insisted they go on. Smokey noticed a new gentleness in her attitude toward Curly. Now she scolded him for taking such a chance. The rider's keen ears overheard her say, "Why, if you'd had a sore or cut in your mouth, we'd have been missing a driver."

"Would you care?"

Smokey lingered until he caught a low "Yes," then smiled and rode off to watch the cattle and extra horses.

Within a week, Mrs. Cook had taken up the duties Rebecca, Conchita, and Curly shared to give her extra rest. Her friends rejoiced, drawn closer than ever by the near tragedy averted by a brave and loving man.

Now, every day brought them nearer to their goal. While the sun still shone brightly, summer began to wane. Autumn gave its warning with cooling nights and a rainstorm now and then. They reached Phoenix but didn't linger. With more than four hundred miles, they had come two-thirds of the way. Yet mountains and valleys, canyons and rivers stretched before them, to be crossed before a possible early snowfall made the going treacherous.

As Smokey rode his faithful Buckskin, curiosity about what lay ahead and whether it could fill his unspoken longing possessed him. He thrilled at the strange red-rock formations Joel had described, at the deep canyons, brilliant blue sky, and blazing white stars that looked close enough to pick from a tall ladder. He rose to the challenge of climbing from the bowels of the earth, like the swooping eagles, to the heights of stony promontories. With every step of his horse's hooves, Arizona sang a song so beguiling, someday he vowed to claim it for his own.

CHAPTER 3

Blue shadows lay heavy in the Tonto Basin. Evening had fallen and with it a hush after the warm summer day. Desert birds slowed, then stilled their twittering songs and prepared for the night. A myriad of great, shining stars waited in the wings to be summoned when the shadows deepened.

Blue shadows lay faint but discernible against the translucent skin of a sleeping girl, mute witness that life in her beloved country was not always kind. Her gently rounded cheek, streaked with the dried streams of tears, rested on a pillow of soft moss. The worst outlaw in the Arizona Territory could not help but note the innocence of the sweet face and the helplessness of the slight body.

As a full yellow moon chased away the lingering shadows, creatures of the night yawned and came into their own. Yet neither the scurry of clawed feet nor the distant cry of a coyote wailing for his mate disturbed the sleeper. Not until the stealthy step of something foreign to her surroundings — signaled by the breaking of a twig — did she open her eyes.

A single motion, like that of a frightened doe, brought her upright, crouched, alert for danger. Fair hair, further silvered by the moon, waved back over her small ears, and tendrils loosened by sleep brushed her cheeks. "Who is it?" Her whisper sounded loud in the suddenly silent night.

"Aw, Colley, it's just me." A dark-haired man stepped into the open and doffed his sweat-stained sombrero.

"Hadley, how dare you creep up on me like this!" Fear gave way to anger. Young as she might be, she could handle her stepfather's right-hand man. "And don't call me Colley. I hate it. My name is Columbine, if you must call me anything at all." She turned to leave, moccasined feet quick on the needle-covered ground.

The man stepped in front of her. His eyes looked like dark holes beneath furry charcoal brows. "C'mon, Coll-Columbine, don't get mad. The only way I can see you is like this. That daddy of yores don't cotton to anyone hanging 'round you, except maybe himself." He laughed coarsely. "I'm a heap sight younger and better looking than he is. Why don't we run off and get hitched?"

In spite of her frail appearance, seventeen-year-old Columbine Ames, named for the Rocky Mountain columbine, which matched her expressive blue eyes, possessed the pioneer spirit of her late father. Josiah Ames had traveled with his wife and child to the Arizona Territory from Colorado only to fall victim to spotted fever. Desolate and alone, his beloved girl-bride had to raise their only child in a raw and wild country. Grim determination to hang on saw mother and daughter through until three years ago, when Caroline Ames remarried.

"Zeke is my stepfather," she answered haughtily. "He worshiped Mother."

"And yore the spittin' image of her," Hadley reminded. He took a step closer. "You and yore fancy house he built for you and yore ma, you think yore too good for me. Haw haw, I could tell you things —"

"I'm not interested in anything you have to say," Columbine interrupted. Yet the vague misgivings she had felt ever since her mother died washed over her until she felt weak. No time to consider them now. She had to get away from Hadley. She'd caught a whiff of his breath when he came toward her and shuddered. Men could be beasts when they drank. Her mother had taught her that long ago, carefully protecting the girl from the wild men who lived in the brakes and had secret stills far back in the canyons. Even Zeke . . .

"Move out of the trail, please." Her heart thumped, and she didn't expect her unwilling suitor to obey. To her surprise, he backed away.

"Don't forget what I said about us getting married," he called after her. Her heart beating wildly, Columbine wondered what she would do if he attempted to stop her. Filled with loathing, she didn't deign to reply but instead offered a silent prayer. *I know we aren't to hate others, Lord, but I'm so afraid.* A night bird's plaintive cry sent a pang through her heart. *Why did Mother have to die?* The question persisted, in cadence with her sure feet that barely touched the ground.

Her disquiet grew stronger as she crept into the large, comfortable house Zeke Stockton had built for his wife and her daughter. Too keyed up to sleep, Columbine sat by her window and stared into the night. A crooning wind lulled her, but she refused to give in to its spell or to the hypnotic swaying of the cottonwoods, with their rustling, gossiping leaves.

During the months since her mother's death, something had been growing within her. Until then, she had accepted Zeke Stockton for what he was: a sandy-haired man with rather colorless eyes, fortyish, tall, and heavy-set without being fat. He had been kind to the fourteen-year-old girl he acquired with his bride, and Columbine knew the depths of his love for her frail mother. She had seen it in his face, the way he deferred to his new wife's wishes. But at times, his fierce expression frightened her. Once, one of the mysterious men with whom he had cattle dealings rode in and made the mistake of admiring too openly the fair-haired, blue-eyed Caroline Stockton.

At other times, a kind of anguish filled Zeke's eyes, and Columbine recalled how she had inadvertently stumbled on him a few days after her mother died. The massive shoulders shook. The hard face was contorted with grief. She had made a move to escape, but he had seen her. "It's just you and me now," he said heavily before turning on his boot heel and walking away.

From that moment, a new and disturbing element rose between them. For weeks she had tried to pass it off as shared grief, but more and more Zeke stayed home instead of riding out with the men. He brightened when Columbine entered the room and a dozen times commented, "You're so like her."

Now Hadley's suggestion bit into the girl's mind like salt into a wound. Surely Zeke wouldn't be interested in anyone less than half his age! Did he see in her a replacement for the wife he lost after such a short time? "Dear God, I need Your wisdom," she prayed, glad for the strong faith her parents had instilled in her from the cradle. "If this is true, I'll have to go away."

Where? How? her tired brain asked. Columbine had no answers. She wouldn't be eighteen until July, months away. Even if she were, could she escape if Zeke willed otherwise? The men who rode for him would do as he ordered. Indeed, men like Hadley haunted the trails.

"Why did Father and Mother ever come to this place, anyway?" she despairingly asked the spangled velvet sky. Yet even as she asked no one in particular, she knew the answer. The chance to build a home and life in a new and ruggedly beautiful territory had fired the Ameses with excitement and determination.

Columbine thought of her childhood, a barefoot, happy existence in the poorest of

cabins — all her mother could afford —
made bright by Caroline Ames's resource-
fulness. A single cow, a few chickens, a well-
tended garden, fruit trees whose blossoms
perfumed the air, and a few beehives spelled
home. Mother love and blessings from their
heavenly Father overshadowed a lack of
things. In time their few books grew tat-
tered; Mother's Bible became worn with
hard use. Columbine grew as wild and
unspoiled as fragile flowers that bent with
the storms and yet continued to glorify the
world with their delicate beauty.

She closed her eyes and remembered how
things had changed after Zeke Stockton
came riding by one sunny afternoon. He
appeared thunderstruck to find a slim, attractive woman and young girl living in the
old cabin. Gowned in her favorite sprigged
muslin with flowers that matched the blue
of her eyes, Caroline Ames welcomed him,
made no apology for her humble home, and
offered him buttermilk chilled in the brook
nearby. He came again and again, spruced
up and eager as the cowboys who made eyes
at Columbine on the rare occasions she
visited the towns of Payson or Pine.

When Caroline Ames accepted his offer of
marriage, Zeke promptly made a bold
declaration: "I'll build you the finest home

in this part of Arizona, anywhere you say." Caroline chose a spot nearby, and the little cabin, just out of sight of the main house, became Columbine's refuge. Off-limits to every rider by the iron order of Zeke Stockton, the cabin became a perfect sanctuary for the girl-turning-woman. Now she had a place to read the books Zeke brought home in his saddlebags from Flagstaff, a spot to dream all the dreams of maidenhood triggered by fairy tales and Bible stories of Esther and Ruth.

Often she wondered how she would meet the man God knew could complete her life. Father had met Mother at a barn raising in Colorado. Zeke, of course, had simply been riding by. Sometimes when lying flat on her back and looking through green tree lace at a sapphire sky or watching a lazy trout reject her bait and retreat beneath a rock in the amber water, she whispered her shy secrets to God.

When her mother knew her time on earth had nearly run out, she called Columbine to her side. "Always remember, I'm just ahead of you on the trail, my darling. Although you will be lonely without me, the years before we meet again to spend eternity together are just a twinkling in God's eyes. Trust Him with your whole heart. Honor and glorify Him in all you do." She raised herself up on one thin white arm, and her eyes glowed. "Above all, never marry a man who doesn't love our God with all his heart."

Columbine lifted her swollen face, and a fresh batch of tears gushed down her cheeks. "But Mother, Zeke —"

"I know." An ineffable look of pain darkened Caroline's tired blue eyes. "He has been good to us both, and I care for him a great deal. My final prayer is that one day he will respond to the love of Christ. Somewhere inside Zeke is the divine spark God has put in everyone. He has given me everything I ever wanted, but he has not turned his heart over to God. Be a witness, Darling."

That night when Columbine kissed her good night, she seemed stronger, and the girl's sad heart rejoiced. Perhaps God would spare her precious mother after all, at least for a few more weeks. Yet a few hours later, death released her undying spirit from its wasted body. Zeke and Columbine buried her on a little slope beneath a tall pine where she had sought shade many times.

Too weary for memories that harrowed her soul, Columbine rested her head on her arms. Trust. Honor. Glorify. Witness. God

— and Mother — had laid the path before her. She must travel it warily, triumphantly. She slid into a simple white nightgown and got into bed. That path looked steep and hard, like the climb from the Tonto Basin to the Rim that frowned above it, dark with timber, forbidding and unfriendly. "Dear God, Your Son walked a harder path. Keep my feet, I pray." She fell asleep before she could add, "Amen."

Once suspicious of her stepfather, Columbine took to staying awake nights. Dark riders whose horses' hooves sounded muffled were regular nocturnal visitors at the Cross Z ranch. Zeke had purchased land all around the old Ames cabin and stocked it with cattle and horses, branded with the distinctive Z. Hidden by the thin curtain at her window, Columbine felt no compunction at eavesdropping. A feeling of wrongness had replaced much of the grief and the inner urge to flee from she knew not what.

Now and then heated voices and harsh laughter rose, and she shrank back. Once she heard a shot followed by a cry. The next day she asked her stepfather about the shooting.

Zeke sat still, his eyes blank. "It woke you?"

"Yes."

"One of the boys had a bit too much," he told her nonchalantly. "Fired at an owl."

She said no more, but paralyzing fear swept through her. No owl had made the cry in the night. More than ever, she knew she must find out what was going on. Impulsively, she turned to Zeke and said, "Father, men didn't come in the night when Mother was alive."

A wave of unaccustomed red rose in his face. His lips tightened, then relaxed. "No, Columbine." A strange laugh erupted from his mouth, one that frightened her. "I get lonely. It helps to have the men in." He rose and patted her fair hair with his meaty hand. "You're more like her every day," he mumbled, then jerked his hand away and strode out.

New dread attacked her. If Zeke were confusing her and her mother in his mind, what would happen? She shivered in spite of the warm day. That night for the first time in her entire life, she wished she had a lock on her bedroom door.

Yet as falling leaves changed from green to gold, no further incidents occurred. Zeke was going away on a cattle deal for a few days, to her relief. Mounted and ready, with Hadley grinning from behind him, Zeke said, "Andy Cullen's staying to look after

71

you. He sprained an ankle when his horse slammed him against the corral."

"Wish I'd athought of that," Hadley smirked.

Zeke whirled, his face flaming, voice deadly. "What's that supposed to mean?"

"Not a thing, Boss." But Columbine caught his sideways look and knew he lied.

"It better not." Zeke glanced toward Columbine, his face dark with fury. "She has the deadliest rifle in Arizona and knows how to use it. She won't hesitate, should any polecat or other varmint bother her." Hadley paled and rode off without another word, closely followed by the rest of the outfit.

Zeke lingered a moment. "Yell for Andy if you need to. Otherwise, stay away from the bunkhouse. If something hadn't come up, I'd have found a woman to come in."

Her laughter pealed out unnaturally. "Really, Father. I don't need anyone. I'm almost a woman." She regretted her words the moment she said them.

He paused, rolled a cigarette and lighted it, then slowly said, "I know. When we get back, I want to talk to you." Putting spurs behind his horse, Zeke headed after the others.

Waving good-bye, Columbine clutched at

her last shreds of self-control and wondered again what she was going to do.

That evening, Andy hobbled over from the bunkhouse. Not much older than Columbine, he was the newest hand hired and her favorite. The first few months he'd worked at the Z, he showed every evidence of wanting to spark her. Once he'd gone so far as to waylay her outside the cabin and lay his hands on her shoulders. His shock of corn-colored hair tossed in the breeze, and his brown eyes teased. "Miss Columbine, will you be my girl?"

Her first indignant reaction gave way to understanding. In Andy's simple code, both of them were young and unattached. What could be more natural than their drifting together? Yet Columbine's inner sense whispered this nice young man didn't fit the image of her future husband. She slipped from his light grip and looked straight into his eyes. "Andy, I don't want to be your girl, but I do want to be your friend. Will you let me?"

Chivalry of the range had been born and bred into him. His hands dropped to his sides. "I'll be proud to be your friend, Miss Columbine." He couldn't help adding, "Who knows? Maybe someday you'll change your mind."

After a few talks, along with the lack of opportunity to see each other because of Stockton's vigilant guarding, not to mention the arrival of a new rancher with a pretty daughter, Andy slid from would-be sweetheart to staunch friend.

Columbine watched him come, salving her conscience with the fact Zeke had said nothing about visiting Andy on the front porch. "Laid up, I see," she greeted him when he sat down on the top step and leaned back against a post so he could watch her while they talked.

"Yeah." He acted jumpy, not like himself at all. Trouble shone from his brown eyes.

"What's wrong, Andy?"

"I wish I knew." The teasing light she saw so much in his young face wasn't there tonight. "Miss Columbine, have you ever thought of getting clean away from the Cross Z?"

Her face betrayed their kindred feelings. She smoothed the skirt of the simple blue housedress she had made and wore evenings. "Why would you ask such a thing?" She quickly pushed aside the wild notion that perhaps she hadn't succeeded in dampening his caring and this was a hint about eloping. A quick glance under long lashes clearly showed whatever was bothering

Andy had nothing to do with romance.

"Sometimes I see and hear things."

"Such as?" She abandoned her rigid pose and leaned forward.

He rumpled his hair until he resembled a wild man in one of Columbine's books. "Little things."

"What *little* things?" she persisted.

He looked at her doubtfully, as if weighing whether to speak or button his lip.

"If I need to know anything, I'd appreciate your telling me," she said quietly.

"I reckon it ain't my place, but you've been so nice and friendly." A wave of red crept into his tanned face. "Uh, has Hadley — or anyone — been bothering you?"

She gasped, feeling someone had poured cold creek water over her. "Hadley followed me once and made some comments about — about —"

"About your daddy who ain't?" The red mounted higher.

Columbine's heart fell with a sickening thud. If Andy had noticed Zeke's interest, the thing she feared must be real.

"I hate like sin asking you," Andy burst out. "But he's too old, and no matter how much he thinks so, you just ain't your mother." Misery filled his eyes.

"Just lately I've wondered." She faltered

75

and could not continue. Her hands nervously pleated and unpleated a fold of her dress. Did she dare ask Andy what she dreaded? Who else could she ask, except God? She bit her lip. "Y-you don't think he means bad by me, do you?" She felt her cheeks go scarlet.

Andy leaped to his feet, white-faced and heedless of his sore ankle. "By all that's holy, he'd better not!" He towered over her, the male protecting the weaker sex. Gradually his body relaxed, and he sat down again and absently rubbed his ankle. "It's more likely he wants to marry you."

"Marry me?" If her heart hadn't felt like lead, Columbine would have screamed with laughter at the absurd idea. "Impossible!"

Andy shook his head. "Any man would be proud to marry you," he said slowly with a twinkle in his brown eyes. "Well, any man but me. Since I done asked you a couple of times and you said no, why, I'm just your friend Andy."

"Besides, you have another girl," she put in, trying desperately to still the trembling of her lips.

A new manliness enveloped his countenance. " 'Course, if it meant getting married in order to save you, that would be a whole new game."

76

"Andy, Dear," she choked out. "You'll never know how good it is to have a friend like you. I won't take advantage of your offer, no matter what happens, but someday I may have to call on you for help."

He stood, held out a hand, and kept hers when she rose. With a solemn expression in his eyes, he vowed, "It won't have to be more than a whisper, Miss Columbine." With a gentle pressure, he released her hand and went down the steps and across to the bunkhouse, a gallant, limping figure Columbine saw through a blur. Andy was not a storybook knight but a flesh-and-blood cowboy the girl knew had been sent to the Cross Z by a loving God.

CHAPTER 4

The week Stockton and his men were gone from the Cross Z offered a sunlit valley of peace in the midst of Columbine's mountains of trouble. A strain of music composed by the Master Author ran through the land, played and sung by whispering trees, swaying grass, a multitude of birds, little brooks, and a capricious breeze.

After the first night when Andy promised to stand by Columbine if the need arose, neither said more about it. There would be time enough to plot the future when Stockton and his dark riders returned. For now, Columbine was enjoying the simple pleasures of having her first true friend.

Most of Columbine's life had been spent away from others her own age. Her mother had taught her at home, and visits to Payson and Pine were few and far between. Andy, however, had been on his own since he turned fifteen. Skilled in range lore, he

78

carried his weight on the Cross Z as well as the older men, although he knew Stockton had only hired him because many cowboys wanted to work closer to town.

"Doesn't bother me." He shrugged. "I never cared about drinking and playing cards."

"How can you get along with Hadley and the others?" the curious girl asked, watching the stream ripple over stones at her feet, while Andy lounged nearby, favoring his ankle.

"Mind my own business and keep out of his way." Cullen's boyish lips set hard. "He would have fired me by now except your daddy, uh, Stockton wouldn't hear of it." A glint turned the brown eyes amber. "I heard him tell Hadley to lay off 'the kid' 'cause I could shoot the eye out of a needle and the time might come I'd be handy."

"You would never kill a man, would you?" She shrank from him in horror. "It's wrong to kill. Mother taught me from the Bible that God commanded people not to kill."

Andy sat up straight. "I can tell you this. I ain't going to kill anyone on Stockton's account, even if I do work for him." His eyes turned to molten gold, hard and determined. "I can't say for sure I wouldn't shoot

79

a man if he harmed, uh, someone I cared about."

"Andy," she cried, her blue eyes dark with fear. "Promise me that no matter what, you won't do such a terrible thing."

"Aw, why are we talking about killing on such a beautiful day?" He leaned back against a big rock. "Say, have you ever been to Flagstaff? That place is growing to be quite a town. There's a big department store named Babbitt's . . . might be a fine place for a girl to work, if she ever wanted to." He half closed his eyes and winked at her.

Columbine knew her efforts to make him promise had proved futile. She longed for Andy to know God, but wisely she refrained from preaching. Instead she would pray for him and for God-given chances to speak of Him, "plant a seed," her mother had called it. She forced herself to respond to his change of subject. "Next summer after I'm eighteen, do you think I might get a job at Babbitt's?"

"Why not?" He grinned and ruffled his hair in his typical gesture. "A pretty girl behind the counter would be the best reason in Arizona for cowpokes just aching to spend their money, wouldn't it?"

She laughed and refused to rise to his bait, but long after night fell, the idea surged through her. What if she did go to Flag and get work? What would Zeke do? She wouldn't put it past him to follow her, but once she passed her eighteenth birthday, any claim he made would be worthless. Her spirits rose. Zeke Stockton didn't have a claim on her now; he wasn't blood kin. Too bad she didn't have an uncle or aunt or grandparent somewhere. She'd slip away before Zeke came back. A deep sigh escaped her lips. She didn't have anyone except God and Andy. The next minute, she smiled. With God on her side, how could she fail, especially with Andy thrown in for good measure?

But once Zeke came back, she wouldn't even have Andy. Her stepfather would never stand for her new friend to be hanging around. Her lips trembled. Why must life be so hard? She remembered asking her mother that question long ago. Caroline Stockton's quick answer still burned into her brain as if seared with a red-hot branding iron.

"Sometimes I feel that if everything here were perfect, children of God would grow satisfied. . . . They'd stop longing for their real home, the one He has prepared for us." Her blue eyes so like her daughter's took on a faraway look. "Perhaps we would forget how important it is to live according to His plan, not our own."

The thrum of distant hooves warned the two friends, and Columbine gracefully sprang to her feet. Her heart was pounding. "Go, Andy. If Zeke catches you here with me, he may —"

"I'm not afraid of him." The daring cowboy got up more slowly, his brown eyes blazing.

"Please. Just go. You're the only friend I have except God." Frantically, she pushed him toward the bunkhouse.

Her plea did what fear could not. By the time the band of dark-faced, dark-clad riders swung past the woodsy spot, Andy was lounging on the bunkhouse porch whittling. Columbine had fled into the house, whispered a quick prayer, and seated herself, then snatched up a book, feeling deceitful.

"Ho, where's my daughter?" a familiar voice boomed. "Cullen, do you have any idea where she is?"

"I haven't seen her come out of the house since she went in." His laconic reply floated in an open window, and the girl stifled a giggle. Andy had a knack of clinging to the truth in a way that disclosed nothing.

Heavy steps crossed the porch. The door was flung open, and Zeke Stockton, dusty and trail weary, stepped inside. "Fine thing,

when a man can't even get a decent welcome home."

"Hello." She dropped the book and rose.

"Why didn't you come out?" He eyed her
suspiciously, and she felt the color leave her
face at the half-hidden look in his eyes.

"I don't like to be around the men any
more than I have to," she told him truthfully.

"Have any of them dared touch you?" His
voice could have been heard on the streets
of Payson.

"No." Thank God it was true. Even Hadley hadn't laid hands on her, and she didn't
consider the teasing clasp Andy had once
attempted important. "I–I just feel uncom-
fortable around them."

"Did Cullen bother you while I was
gone?"

She shook her head violently. "Oh, no."
Far from it, her heart added. *If he hadn't been
here, I would never have felt I had a chance
of escape. Now I do.*

"How about a welcome home kiss, Colley?" Zeke laughed carelessly, but again his
eyes spoke volumes.

She steeled herself. *God, help me.* "Father." She hesitated. She'd seldom called
him that, even when he'd asked her to.
"Father, I'm getting too old for that."

He flinched as if struck. "Oh, you are, are you?"

For a moment, she didn't know what he'd do, so she added, "Yes. I'll be eighteen next summer." She hated to remind him after what he had told her when he left but saw no other choice. "I'm not a little girl."

At a loss for words, Zeke regained his composure the next instant by bursting into a laugh. "Spunky, aren't you? Good. Your mother was, too." A peculiar softness stole into his colorless eyes, creating more fear in Columbine than when he raged.

"I'm not Mother," she reminded, forcing herself to be gentle, although her hands were clenched tightly behind her blue-checked gown.

The softness fled, and Stockton's face turned to granite. He abruptly turned. "I have to get cleaned up." Polished floorboards creaked under his weight, and Columbine heaved a sigh of relief as a daring idea hovered and opened its wings. She appeared at supper with her hair in two plaits the way she had worn it as a child, wearing a dress as different from anything her mother had worn as possible.

"What have you done to yourself?" Zeke eyed her with disfavor. "You don't look right. I like your hair the other way."

Because Mother never had plaits. Columbine forced herself to laugh. "I just thought it might be cooler this way."

"I still don't like it." He rested his knife and fork on his plate and continued to stare.

Her plan had failed, but fortunately, after a long time in prayer, another had come. "Father, you'll never know how happy Mother would be that you've always treated me like your own daughter. You've fed me and clothed me, given me books, and made sure no one pestered me." She glanced down and risked a quick glance at him from beneath her lashes. "You're the only father I can remember, and no one could have been kinder."

A line seemed to form around Zeke's mouth, and his jaw set. Would reminding him of Mother and how she trusted herself and her young daughter to his care reach the good in him? Was Zeke's heart waiting to be kindled to the love of Christ?

She played her trump card. "Did you ever think God sent you to us so I could have a father?"

Stockton turned chalky. Suddenly, he leaped to his feet, sending his chair crashing backward to the floor. One great fist slammed into his other hand, and he staggered as if mortally wounded, then lurched

85

out the door.

Columbine heard his unsteady progress across the porch and ran to the window that gave full view of the corral and bunkhouse. She covered her ears at the curses he had never used in front of her or her mother, curses she knew only from overhearing the cruder hands.

"Give me that!" Zeke snatched a lariat from Andy Cullen, who sat perched on the corral fence coiling his rope. It whistled and dropped over a feisty stallion's neck. Iron hands reined in the dancing horse and put saddle and bridle in place. In one fluid motion, Zeke leaped to the steed's back. "Open the gate," he bellowed.

Andy scrambled to obey. Stockton and his wild-eyed mount sprang through and thundered out of sight.

The watching girl felt she had been wrung dry. She groped her way to a chair, and her knees buckled. She hadn't known what to expect, but this? "The way he acted shows he doesn't think of me as a daughter," she whispered brokenly. "He never will again. What can I do?" She rocked back and forth like a grieving child. A dozen plans came to mind, but she rejected them all. If she vanished now, Zeke would know she had realized his feelings for her had changed.

Somehow she managed to clear away the supper neither of them had more than tasted. Listlessly, she washed the dishes and rinsed out her dish towels and hung them to dry. In the weeks after her mother's death, Columbine had sturdily insisted she could keep the house and needed no help. Now she bitterly regretted it. Was it too late to ask Zeke to hire a woman, a motherly soul who could serve as shield and comfort? But who? All the women in that category that they knew either had families of their own or were comfortably situated in Pine or Payson.

"It would take time," she murmured and slowly went to her room. As on other clear nights, she sat by the window for a long time. Unable to sleep, she neither undressed nor thought of going to bed, even when pointing shadows crept into her pretty room. Finally she rose, slipped out of the large house that oppressed her, and fled into the night on moccasined feet. Silent as a mountain lion on padded feet, she wended her way toward her mother's grave. The sight that greeted her froze her in her tracks. Bare-headed, his massive head in his arms, Zeke Stockton was kneeling by the grave.

Columbine sank to the ground, glad for the whispering cottonwoods that would disguise any noise she might make, unwilling to retreat for fear she'd been seen or heard. A prayer for her stepfather formed in her heart, a petition that in his loss he wouldn't turn to the only living part of his beloved dead wife. Perhaps one day, she prayed, he would give his heart to the Lord Jesus Christ, the only One who could heal Zeke's agony.

In the next few days, she sensed the struggle in his soul between nobility — a strange word to apply to a man such as Zeke Stockton — and desire. If she had seen such a look in Hadley's face, it would have repulsed her and sent her fleeing in horror. Oddly enough, the new understanding Columbine had that Zeke saw her not as a young girl but as her mother blocked hatred. Yet when he rode away for a day and Andy, now healed and back working, managed to talk with her, new worries arose.

"I don't know what's up, but it ain't good," the honest cowboy admitted. He shot a questioning glance at her. "Have you heard anything?"

"I think he's going to have a huge fall roundup and sell off most of our cattle and horses," Columbine said. She wrinkled her forehead, trying to piece together snatches of conversation between Zeke and Hadley, who had become a nightly visitor at the house. Sometimes other men came, too, but Hadley was always there. She had all she could do to keep out of his way, hating the boldness in his face every time she met him.

"Can you stand some bad news?"

Her heart lurched. "Why, yes."

Andy glanced both ways. "The Cross Z ain't got all that many cattle and horses. I've been riding the brakes."

"Maybe he's going to buy and resell." She knew it to be false before he shook his head.

"That doesn't make a lot of sense, what with winter coming on. A roundup's to do just that. Round up critters you don't want to keep over the winter."

"Then how — ?" She choked on her words.

"Do you really have to ask?" Andy glanced away.

She shook her head, too stunned to speak. For the first time, she felt fiercely thankful for her mother's death, thankful that her mother had not realized her husband was a rustler.

"I didn't know if I should say anything. It's enough to make a person bawl like a spooked steer." Sympathy darkened his eyes to almost black. "Maybe you think it's pretty rotten of me to squeal, but I promised to be your friend, and one of these days, there's going to be a fight like you never saw before." Gloom laced every word. "Miss Columbine, ain't there some way you can get out of here? I'll take you, if I can. I don't aim to stick around much longer. I'd have gone soon as I heard about the stinking mess Stockton's in if it hadn't been for you."

The truth beat against her like branches whipping in a gale. Her mouth went dry. Columbine Ames, trapped in a nest of rustlers. No wonder Hadley had sneered when he accused her of thinking she was too good for him. No wonder he'd said he could tell her things! Had her inner awareness even then recognized and refused to listen to unspoken evil? "I–I don't think I can bear it," she whispered.

"Aw, sure you can," Andy comforted. "Look how the flowers you're named for bend in the wind. Yet they keep right on blooming and growing, don't they?" He shuffled his boots on the needle-covered ground. "Maybe it ain't as bad as I think, but I'd keep my eyes peeled and ears open." He pressed his lips in a straight line. "And my door locked."

Fresh fear gripped her. "I don't have a lock on my door."

"Then stick a chair under the knob. I

don't trust Hadley any more than a polecat."
Red rushed into Andy's clear face, but his
gaze never left hers.

"You haven't heard anything, have you?"
she demanded.

"Just that he's loco over you and telling
the rest of the men he'll skin them like rab-
bits if they get any ideas. Uh, have you had
any trouble with Z— uh, with anyone else?"

She knew he had started to say "Zeke."
"No."

"Good. Then keep your door locked and
your chin up. I'll get you out of here somehow, no matter what it takes." He grinned
and headed back to work before anyone
could see and suspect him.

That night Zeke Stockton rode in, somber
and sullen. All through supper he watched
her. To her excited fancy, he appeared to be
suspicious of her. Could Hadley or some of
the others have reported her talk with Andy?
Or was it merely the battle between good
and evil waging war in his soul?

She started to rise and clear the table.

"Sit down, Columbine."

She'd never heard him speak in that tone.
Tongues of dread licked at her. "I–I just
thought I'd get the dishes done before the
men come in."

"They won't be coming tonight. Not even

Hadley." Light from the lamp she had lit against the early dusk glittered in his eyes, making them more unreadable than ever. "I've thought about it considerable, and I won't wait any longer to speak. Your mother's been gone a year." A spasm of pain contracted the muscles of his face but didn't stop him from continuing. For as long as she lived, Columbine would see his face in the flickering lamplight and relive the gorge that rose within her.

"Hadley's after you. So are half the others. I want you to marry me. You'll be safe, and I'll take care of you." He never took his gaze from her.

She remained silent long enough to ask a prayer for help. What she said now would change the course of her life. She raised her head. "Zeke, you honor me by asking." She struggled to find words that would not antagonize him, her hands clenched until the knuckles showed white against her sprigged gown. "I know I look and act like Mother and —"

"It isn't all that." He leaned forward, hope in his face. "I admire you for yourself, too, Colley. I guess I could even say I love you."

"Thank you for saying that. Father, Zeke, Mother taught me I must never marry any man I don't love with all my heart," she managed to get out.

"You'd come to it in time," he said gruffly. "She loved me that way, didn't she?"

Feeling the ground shake beneath her, Columbine told him, "Yes, she did."

"There can't be anyone else for you," he pondered. "I've seen to that."

"There's no one else. It's just that I know I don't love you in the right way. Zeke, I still think of you as the father who came along when I was a girl. Can't we leave it that way?" Something flickered in his eyes, and she dared hope.

"Maybe all you need is time," he said stubbornly. "What if we forget about it for now and talk again later?"

The temptation to agree nearly over-whelmed her, yet she dared not give in. "I don't think I'll change."

"You might." He stood and laughed. It took every ounce of courage she possessed to keep from shrinking away from him. "I can give you everything you'll ever want," he said, not boasting but stating facts. "If you'd rather live in town, I'll sell out and build there, in Payson or Pine, not Flag." His face darkened. "I'm getting tired of living here in the brakes. How'd you like for me to do one last drive and take you somewhere else, say Colorado or maybe Wyoming?"

Columbine's nails bit into her palms. Andy's direful predictions were on target.

The clink of spurs in the doorway saved her from the need to answer or commit herself. "Sorry to interrupt, Boss, but the, uh, rancher who wants to buy stock's here." Hadley's leer in her direction set the girl's cheeks burning.

"I've told you never to come in here without knocking." Zeke's deadly voice turned even Hadley's face pale. "Now get out."

"Yeah, Boss, but your *visitor* says he's in a hurry." With a last meaningful look, Hadley disappeared into the night.

Stockton followed him, leaving his coveted stepdaughter alone in the room. Columbine knew she must get away, but unless God sent a miracle, she was trapped.

CHAPTER 5

Several uneasy days passed. Columbine continued with her household duties, unchanged on the outside. Inwardly, she trembled with the growing certainty of her stepfather's crooked dealings. Now that her eyes had been opened, little things she had passed over as insignificant loomed large and frightening. The night visits. The card playing, drinking, and loud voices.

From the fragile safety of her bedroom, chair faithfully propped beneath the doorknob, the girl so like a flower listened and feared, hoped and dreamed, and prayed for the day she could leave. Sometimes she believed Zeke could read her mind. In any event, he assigned Andy Cullen to night guard over the cattle and his henchmen to watch her like a hawk during the day. She had no opportunity for a word with her cowboy friend. Only her strong faith in God's deliverance helped her bear her situation.

To worsen matters, Hadley never missed an opportunity to cast his bold glance her way when Stockton wasn't looking. She refused to let him intimidate her and coolly met his gaze. The biding-my-time glint in his dark, predatory eyes spoke more clearly than words his resentment that a common rustler's daughter should scorn him.

Zeke also bided his time. Although Columbine knew he seldom let her out of his sight except when away on cattle deals, he said no more about marriage. His silence offered no consolation. Each time she passed by, furtively he would reach out and touch her full-skirted gown in a tender caress. Yet her heart sank when more and more often she caught the whiff of whiskey on his breath. She longed to cry out, to remind him how much her mother had hated drinking, but she dared not. Any criticism could shatter the undeclared temporary truce between them.

One night, however, the fragile peace was smashed to smithereens. Columbine had seen the usual procession of evening visitors earlier, heard the too-familiar sounds of frontier mirth and argument, followed by loud voices. Unable to sleep, she huddled by her window. One by one, the riders who haunted her dreams as well as her days rode away. A long time later, she heard uneven steps in the hall outside her bedroom door.

There was a fumbling with the knob. "Oh, God, help me," she whispered.

The fumbling continued.

In a frenzy of fear, Columbine snatched a dress, pulled it over her nightgown, and slid her feet into moccasins. She slipped behind the curtains, prepared for flight.

Crash! The door slammed against the wall so hard it shook the floor. A heavy figure stumbled in, groped his way to the empty bed, and fell to his knees.

Columbine seized her only opportunity. Step by cautious step, she inched her way to the open door. Incoherent mumbling told her Zeke still knelt by the bed. Whiskey fumes filled the air. With one hand over her nose, she reached the door.

"Why did you go and leave me?"

Zeke's wild question halted her but only for a second. Pity mingled with fear, and she knew he again had confused her with her mother. With noiseless steps, she went down the hall, her mind strangely clear. Zeke was in no condition to follow her. Even if he called for whatever cowboys weren't on night watch, she still had a margin of time. She hurried to the kitchen, glad for the knowledge that allowed her to skirt furniture and forage in cupboards and pantry. The rest of the supper roast. Cold biscuits. A large chunk of cheese. She would get water from the creek. Into the living room she dashed for a blanket, and her preparations ended. Supplies knotted in a dish towel she could use as a knapsack, blanket over her light dress and fair hair, she reconnoitered at the front door. Not a sound disturbed the stillness. Not the friendly cry of a night bird, not the rustle of small animals scurrying about their nocturnal business. A quick step brought her to the porch, but instead of crossing it and going down the steps, she turned and walked its length and stepped to the ground at the side of the house and thanked God.

Where should she go? Not to her mother's grave. Zeke would look there first. She struck out from the large house toward her cabin refuge. Did she dare go inside, bolt the door, and pray for safety? In spite of his order, Zeke in his alcoholic condition would break his own rule unless he went into a stupor. She walked on until she reached the shady spot by the stream where she and Andy had spent such happy hours. It seemed a lifetime had passed since then, but it had been just a few weeks. Taking advantage of the starlight that cast a dim glow and provided black shadows beneath the cottonwoods, Columbine managed to put a few miles between her and the house. She wondered if her stepfather had missed her . . . perhaps he was still crying for his dead wife. In either case, she couldn't take a chance.

She crept on, not knowing where she could go and be safe. She reached the spot where Hadley had accosted her and glanced fearfully at the bushes as if expecting them to rustle. Her eyes opened wide. Was it her imagination, or had something moved behind her? Too late she whirled. Strong fingers cut off her cry for help, and a steel arm pinioned her own arms to her body. She fought to no avail. The unknown assailant pulled her off the trail into deep shadows. Silently she prayed, *Deliver me from evil.*

"Lie still," her captor whispered. "Hadley's after you."

The throbbing of her heart left her lightheaded. *Andy.* Andy Cullen had snatched her from harm. Too relieved to wonder why or how he'd found her, she sagged against his arm. He removed his other hand from her mouth but only after a low warning, "Don't make a move."

A footfall showed how close behind her

Hadley had been. He must have seen her slip from the house. Terror came again, digging claws into her until her body quivered, and Andy gave her arm a reminding squeeze. Long after Hadley's black figure had disappeared and night sounds told them danger had passed, they remained in hiding.

"Come." Andy took her hand and led her back up the trail but cut off in a different direction before they reached the main road to the house. Exhausted more emotionally than physically, Columbine followed, glad for the strong hand that led her. Their strange trek made a curious impression on her. Sometimes she heard the ripple of water and knew they traveled near the brook. At other times they traversed open spaces between clumps of trees, bent low and moving slowly. Hours later, they stopped before what looked like a vast dark hole. "You'll be safe here," Andy told her.

Columbine's sight had adjusted to the starlight. "A cave. How did you find it?"

He didn't answer until they went inside. "Ever since we talked about your having to get away, I've been looking for someplace you could stay if you needed to." His gruff voice couldn't hide his anger. "Here." He took the blanket from her shoulders and wrapped it more securely around her. "There's another on the ground so we can sit."

She gratefully dropped to the cave floor. Enough light came from a small opening in the ceiling to the right of where they sat so she could discern his set face. "Andy, how did you happen to be here when I needed you so much?"

"Maybe that God of yours sent me." He shrugged. "I've been feeling uneasy the last few nights. Tonight when I got the herd bedded down and could see the other night guards were eager to spin yarns around the fire, I said I'd just as lief mosey around and keep an eye out. They called me a fool but laughed and told me some jaspers were suckers for punishment. I've been watching the house, just in case . . ." His voice trailed off. "What happened tonight, anyway?"

"Zeke had been drinking. If he hadn't, I know he never would have broken into my room."

Andy leaped to his feet. "I'll kill him for that!" His low voice rang deadly against the cave walls.

"No," she told him desperately. "He didn't hurt me. He didn't even think of me, just of Mother. Andy, even if it weren't wrong to kill, suppose you shot Zeke? Hadley and the others would either shoot or hang you, and where would I be then?"

"Out of the branding-iron fire and into a forest fire, I reckon." Andy sat back down, breathing hard.

"I need you alive," she told him. "Besides, I honestly don't think Zeke will harm me unless he's so far gone with whiskey he doesn't know what he's doing."

"What are you going to do now?" he demanded.

Her thoughts spun like a singing lariat. "Stay here for a day or two. I brought food. I want you to go back to the herd right away, before someone misses you. Then tomorrow, see what happens at the ranch. The men will be bound to talk. If you can get away tomorrow night for a little while, come tell me what you've learned."

"Leave you here alone? Suppose your friend Hadley finds you?"

"He won't. There's no reason for him to look here, is there? How many of the men know about this cave?" Yet his suggestion chilled her, and she drew the warm blanket closer about her body.

"Any of them could, but there ain't much reason for them to," he admitted. "I stumbled on it by chance when I was chasing a maverick."

102

"Chance?" her soft, sweet voice challenged. "Or did God lead you here?"

He hunched his shoulders and wrapped his arms around his drawn-up knees. "Might not be such a bad idea at that." With a slight spring, he stood, a lithe defender. "You probably won't need this, but just in case a mean critter wants the cave, I'll feel better if you have it on hand." He pulled something heavy and cold from his shirt and placed it in her hands. "It's loaded. Use it if you have to." A few strides took him to the mouth of the cave. "Stay holed up inside except when you go for water. The creek's straight down and not far. I'll see you tomorrow night or the next at the latest."

She wanted to cling to him, to beg him not to go, but her pioneer stock permitted no weakness. "God bless you, Andy," she called softly. The next moment his dark shape moved, and a large patch of starlight appeared where he had been.

All night Columbine prayed, until sheer fatigue and worry overcame her, and she fell into a deep, dreamless sleep on the earthen floor of the cave. She awakened to the trill of birds and full sunlight, plus the chill of early morning autumn air in the Tonto. Ravenous, hope welling in her heart now that daylight had driven night shadows away, she carefully surveyed the area and satisfied herself no intruder lurked near. The cool water in the stream offered both refreshment and a chance to bathe. Never had food tasted better than the butterless sandwich she made from a cold biscuit, a piece of roast she tore off with her hands, and a sharp, tangy chunk of cheese.

Mindful of Andy's instructions, she stayed near the cave. She whiled away the long hours by seeking out and erasing every footprint that might betray her hiding place. She wished for her Bible, repeating as many promises for deliverance she could remember, and sprang to her feet with a little cry when Andy finally came.

Excitement filled his face. His brown eyes flashed. "Everything's broke loose on the Cross Z," he reported. At the same time, he took from the capacious pockets of his jacket two apples, a chunk of cake carefully wrapped in a clean handkerchief, and two dill pickles. "All I could swipe," he cheerfully told her.

Columbine bit into a juicy apple. "Mmm. Delicious."

"Want to hear what's going on at the ranch?" Andy tormented. His corn-colored hair looked more disheveled than ever.

"Do I!" She finished the apple and

reached for the piece of cake.

"First off, I got back to the herd and checked in with the hands around the fire. None of them was any wiser, so I headed for the bunkhouse at first light. Never saw such a sight." Andy slapped his jeans leg in glee. "Place was lit up like the Fourth of July, men running around like scared prairie chickens.

"Hadley comes bellowing up to me with Stockton right behind him. 'Cullen, have you seen Colley?' " The cowboy's open face clouded. "I wanted to poke him one for not being more respectful."

"Don't stop for that," she begged. She could almost see the vivid scene Andy described.

" 'Miss Columbine?' sez I. 'I just rode in off night duty.'

" 'And yore sure you didn't see her on the way in?' sez he.

" 'Ump-umm.' I *didn't* see you on my way in but on your way out," he chortled. "Anyway, he ups and tells me what he'll do if I'm lying, so I get all wide-eyed and innocent and say, 'She ain't lost, is she, Boss?' I never saw Stockton look so worried as when he barked, 'We hope not. Maybe she just went for an early morning walk, but it's not like her to be late with fixing breakfast.' "

Andy looked disgusted. "I about spilled the beans and said it wasn't any morning walk that made you leave, but instead, I just yawned and said if they needed me to hunt, I'd be glad to. Stockton stared at me for a minute and said no. Told me to get some shut-eye so I could night herd again to-night."

"You said he looked worried."

"Yeah, and dead sober. Your little escapade just about shocked him out of his boots. The way I figure, if you stay out one more night, he will be so miserable and guilty, it will be safe enough for you to go home tomorrow." He scratched his head. "I can't say for how long, though." He hunkered down on his boot heels. "You might want to consider telling him right out he scared you to death coming in your room that way and that you never thought he'd do anything like that."

She rolled it over in her mind, then nod-ded. "I will." The faint hope that rescue lay in appealing to his better side refused to die.

Andy didn't stay much longer. "Can't let anyone miss me," he explained. "Hadley's sorer than a bear with his paw in a trap, and it wouldn't take much for him to draw on me." He grinned sunnily. "Don't worry. I ain't carrying a gun, and even the Cross Z's hard-nut outfit won't stand for him killing me except in a fair fight. Stockton won't, either."

According to arrangement, Columbine spent the second night in the cave, then met Andy at a prearranged spot early the next morning. Andy could truthfully say he found her on the trail while riding in from his night-herding duties. He reported that most of the outfit had been out looking for her. "Good thing you're going in. Sooner or later some sharp-eyed galoot would spot the cave. We don't want that. It may come in handy again."

Their arrival created a sensation. Andy chose to make a grand entrance and sang out, "Here she is!" before he rode in with Columbine behind him. Unshaven men stared, and Hadley's dark face blackened with suspicion. Stockton sprang from his horse. Evidently, he had been about to begin searching again once it got light.

"Colley? Where have you been, Girl?" Relief, shame, guilt, and anger mingled in his broad face.

"Excuse me, Boss, but she's kind of tired and scratched up," Andy put in respectfully, although the runaway knew he had his tongue stuck in his cheek. "Probably hungry, too. Want me to help her in the house and you can talk later?"

"I'll do it." Zeke lifted Columbine down and carried her inside.

She heard Hadley demand, "Where's she been, and where'd you find her? There's something funny about this."

Andy's quick retort floated to her ears. "Nothing funny about getting turned around in the brakes, is there?"

For the umpteenth time, Columbine bit her lip at his clever habit of answering in truthful generalities. She forced herself to lie limp until her stepfather kicked the door shut, then slid from his grasp. She meant to get in first licks. "Father, I never thought you would degrade yourself with drink until I am not safe in my own home."

He stepped back. His mouth dropped open.

Encouraged by the effect of her first shot, she drew herself to her full height, knowing anger would heighten her five feet and a few inches. "I respected you, considered you my protector against the rough men down here who — who . . ." She covered her face with her hands and produced a convincing shudder that completed the sentence. "Now you burst into my room and frighten me until I must flee into the night, to be chased by your men —"

"What's that?" he roared.

"Surely you know Hadley followed me," she lashed out.

"Only to find where you'd gone." His weak defense poured fuel on the fire of her anger, both real and assumed.

"You promised to give me time to consider marriage. Instead, this." She spread her hands in a helpless gesture, one designed to appeal to any remaining sense of decency.

Zeke cried, "I was drunk! I didn't know what I was doing. You don't honestly think I'd hurt you, Colley. You can't believe that." His face whitened. "Why, you're *her daughter.*"

Drained, she had no need to pretend. "I don't know what I believe." Her shoulders drooped. "Now I'd like to bathe and get some rest." She raised her face and looked him squarely in the eyes. "And I'd like a strong bolt put on the inside of my door."

His pallor almost frightened her. "Of course. You won't run away again, will you?" The muscles of his face convulsed.

"Father." She paused. "That all depends on you."

He gasped, but she ignored him and slowly walked away, wondering if the tearing sounds behind her were sobs. With every step came a feeling of security. She had seen in Zeke's eyes what her flight cost him. But she also knew that God had delivered her this time and only He would make a way if the need arose, using methods she might not even know existed.

From the time Zeke Stockton rode into her and her mother's life, Columbine had never seen him show fear. Now it lurked in his face and in the way he treated her. The mysterious night visitors vanished as if they had never been. Zeke made a trip to Flagstaff and came home with bulging saddlebags filled with dress goods, books, and candy. Further, she no longer smelled whiskey on his breath.

Yet even though she could breathe more freely, she knew things couldn't go on as they were. Her power to stave off Zeke's unwelcome attentions wouldn't last forever.

One sunny afternoon, she walked to a secluded part of the little brook where debris from some previous flood had partially dammed the water into a small pool. Not wide enough to swim in, the water came to her waist and offered a sandy bottom. With the privacy afforded by nearby cottonwoods, she decided to bathe and wash her hair.

Columbine sat on a big rock and removed the pins from her sun-kissed hair. How good the creek flowing over amber stones would feel on her skin and hair. She slid out of her moccasins and wiggled her white toes in the narrow stretch of sand beside the pool. Her slender fingers reached for the top button of her blue calico dress.

A rustle in the bushes stopped her. A roar that split the silence of the little glade followed, then wild thrashing, a heavy *thud,* and a dull moan. Frightened, she stared, her hand at her throat.

As if taking a curtain call, the bushes parted and two men hurled toward her.

CHAPTER 6

Eb and Lily Sears stepped from the stage at Flagstaff into the warmest welcome either had ever received. All the slender, dark-eyed woman's fears melted in the quick embrace Judith Scott gave her and the strong hand-clasp from Gideon. Danny, who had been bug-eyed at the sights all the way from Colorado Springs, grinned at the Scott twins. "You're Matt 'n' Millie 'n' Dad says I can have my own pony 'n' maybe you'll teach me to ride 'cause you're three years older 'n' can ride like wild Indians."

His six-year-old hero worship brought instant "Whoopees" from the twins, and they led him to the wagon that would haul them and their parents to the Double J.

As Gideon and Eb joined hands, the long years since their last meeting seemed to melt away. Miles had separated the men as well, since Gideon as a young minister, traveling under his brother's name, rode away from Tomkinsville. He had been cleared of a charge of attempted murder by the man he had outdrawn and whose hand he now held. Eb's face held the eagerness of a boy. "Did you find me a ranch?"

Gideon's blue eyes sparkled in the summer sunlight. "A ranch or a piece of one," he replied. "There's as pretty a little spread not far from the Double J as I've seen. Or you can throw in with the Double J, if you like." Eb started to speak, but Gideon held up a hand. "Don't make up your mind until you see both."

"There's one other thing." Eb glanced at the womenfolk, who had started for the wagon. "Lily has some fool notion she ain't good enough for your wife an' the one Joel's bringin' from Texas. Don't let on I told you, but if you could sorta mention it offhand-like, it'd make everythin' just perfect."

"I will," Gideon promised, and they followed the women. Next to the wagon a fine pair of horses harnessed to a light buckboard pranced restlessly. "Eb, I brought the buckboard in as well as the wagon. How about you and Danny riding in the wagon with me and the twins? Judith can drive Lily and have time to get acquainted."

Lily's dark eyes shone, and Judith's soft smile showed approval of the arrangement.

They drove off in the buckboard, and the others waited until the road dust settled before beginning their journey.

At supper that night, Gideon looked down the long table. "Thank God for having family and friends here," he said simply. "This is truly a time of rejoicing. Dad and Mother have chosen to stay in Arizona. Soon Joel, Cyrus, and their wagon train will arrive, and there will be another grand reunion." He smiled at Judith, then turned to Lily. "My wife had a piano hauled in. Will you sing for us?" He ignored her gasp and the way her face paled. "Lily's one of the spunkiest gals I ever knew and has one of the best voices. She earned our respect by taking care of herself after having to go it on her own, then accepting the chance for something better when it came along." His voice lowered. "The first time I ever saw Lily, I couldn't help thinking it could have been Judith if things had been different."

Gratitude dyed Lily's face a rich color. "If it hadn't been for you and Eb and Joel —"

"God often sends help when we most need it," Gideon said quietly. "Now, no more looking back. We've got a growing number of Christian men, women, and children here in Flag, and we intend to make a difference."

"Please, before you seal the past, may I say something?"

"Of course, Lily."

She met his gaze steadily. "Once you asked if that was my real name and I said no. My name is really Lillian. When I left Tomkinsville, I decided to use it. My first husband and his family liked Lily better. I just wanted you to know I didn't lie." She smiled. "Eb likes it better, too. He says if he had to call me Lillian, I'd have to call him Ebenezer and he'd hate that!" The wave of laughter effectively broke the slight constraint that had fallen on the group. "I'll be happy to sing for you if you'll give me a little time to practice. I haven't done much singing since the Livingstons died. They treated me like their own daughter." Tears glistened in her dark eyes. "It's like you said, though. They'd want me to go on and not look back."

Lige and Naomi had remained silent during the conversation. Now the patriarch's blue eyes held long-remembered pain. "Child, we all have many sad things in our lives that are better put to rest. I certainly have. I just thank God for His goodness and mercy and most of all for His forgiveness. As Gideon said, soon my lost son will be restored to me, even as the son I drove away now sits beside me." His great voice rolled out. "Of all men, I am most blessed. Remember the story in the Bible about the two men who received forgiveness, one a little, one much? And Jesus asked which one would love Him most? Once I begged my older son's forgiveness for my blindness that helped make him what he is, even greater joy than being here came."

Never again did Lily Sears feel anything except what she was, a loved member of the community of Christians bound by gospel cords in a raw new land. But Naomi Scott noticed that more and more often a look of longing crept into her husband's eyes, and he turned his face toward the road on which the wagon train would come.

"The last miles are always the hardest," Joel Scott confided in his friend Smokey one late afternoon shortly before time to make up camp. He had ridden Querida alongside Buckskin when Rebecca chose to keep her adopted father company on the high seat of the wagon he capably drove. As usual, Curly handled the second wagon with Mrs. Cook beside him. Pretty Conchita Perkins sat close to her cowboy husband, Jim, on the third wagon.

"It's grand, isn't it?" Joel's voice fell to a hush.

"Yeah." Smokey couldn't put the feast of colors into words: the cottonwood and willow greens; the turning golden aspens and purple-shadowed canyons; the occasional streams that chuckled over amber rocks; the red buttes and cream-and-black-streaked promontories. "Bet there's fish in some of the creeks we've crossed. Once we get to the Double J and unload, I think I'll take me a little vacation an' come back and see." He grinned in his droll way. "Now, if I were like some folks not so far from here, I'd say this whole little excursion had been a vacation. Such as you an' Rebecca, Jim an' Conchita —"

Joel cut in, blond hair flying, blue eyes filled with mischief. "Don't forget Mrs. Cook and Curly. Have you noticed how she keeps on trying to pretend nothing's changed since he acted so quick when the rattler struck?" He inclined his head toward the buxom, round-faced woman.

Smokey snorted. "Talk about opportunity! Better than in some of those stories writer fellers tell. Just his luck. I could live to be older than one of these Arizona century plants an' not have a chance to shine like that in front of a pretty little filly."

"Cheer up, Smokey." Joel's high spirits spilled over in a loud laugh. "You didn't want to spark Mrs. Cook, did you? She's way too old for you."

Red crept into the cowboy's lean face. He refused to dignify the sally with an answer and broke free to herd one of the plodding cattle back in line.

"Smokey, round up Vermilion for me, will you, please?" Rebecca called from her perch. "I'll ride some more."

Rounding up the red mustang stallion he'd hand-broken with love sent other thoughts flying. The frisky Vermilion took his own sweet time coming when Smokey called, then minced toward him like a coquette at a ball. Finally, the horse sidled up to Buckskin and nuzzled her while Smokey expertly threw a saddle blanket over his back.

"Don't bother with the saddle," Rebecca said. She climbed off the slow-moving wagon. Her booted left foot barely touched Smokey's cupped hands before she swung onto Vermilion and smiled down. "Thanks." Her brown hair and eyes held a reddish glow.

A tiny pang crept into the faithful cowboy's heart. He'd long since overcome any remaining shred of jealousy that might spoil his friendship with Rebecca and Joel. More like a reminder, the hollow place inside him still hadn't been filled. Sometimes when Joel spoke of God and His Son, Smokey felt close to discovering what could take away the empty feeling. Yet he hesitated. He could never be as good as Joel or Rebecca. Probably not as good as Mrs. Cook or even Cyrus Scott, who had brokenly confessed his sinful past to them all a few nights ago.

Smokey sighed, remembering the unashamed tears of his former range boss. Anything that could change the hard rancher once known as Samuel Fairfax into this vulnerable, repentant man must be powerful medicine. He had a feeling that one day soon he'd be taking that medicine. Yet when he considered his life and the need for strength to meet the trouble of which Gideon had written, Smokey balked. Joel mustn't betray his calling, even to clean up a nest of Arizona rattlers. That's where his men would come in, and if a feller hadn't accepted Jesus, who said you had to love your enemies? At this point, he always turned his thoughts elsewhere.

At last the thrilling moment came when the three-wagon train reached Flagstaff. Smokey looked around with interest. "Hmm, some little old town."

Jim Perkins echoed his sentiments. "Snappin' crocodiles, no wonder Joel's been itchin' to get here." He nudged Smokey. "Say, Pard, I don't see no p'rade with girls." He guffawed.

"That's because they didn't know for sure when we'd get here," Smokey loftily told him, to the amusement of the others. "Boss, are we going to stop for supplies and the like?"

Joel hesitated, eyes bluer than ever. "No, let's go home."

Smokey turned away from the poignant light in his friend's face. What would it feel like, having a family waiting? Again the vision of a spread, complete with snug cabin, a light in the window, and a girl running toward him when he came home from herding ornery cows danced before him. The same feeling attacked him again when the wagons reached the crest of the rise and the Double J stretched before them. By mutual and unspoken consent, the drivers halted their horses. Those riding reined in their mounts.

"This is where I came to decide whether I should go or stay," Joel said in a voice little above a whisper.

"Thank God you decided not to stay," Cyrus said raggedly, and Rebecca nodded.

Smokey wondered if he could ever have left had he been Joel. In all their long miles, he had seen no place that struck a chord in his heart the way the Double J did. He could not single out the reason why, yet the whispering yellow-leafed aspens, the rustling grass, and the sighing pine and cedar spelled home. Soon he would know the forested slopes, the peaceful valley, and the red rim-rocked canyons the way he had known northeastern New Mexico. Yet long before he drank his fill of what lay before him, piercing shrieks followed by three horses pelting toward them shattered the silence. Joel slid off his horse and hit the ground running.

"You're here, you're here! Uncle Joel, what took you so long?" Matt and Millie, closely followed by a younger boy Smokey knew must be Danny Sears, slid to a halt. The twins tumbled off and into Joel's bear hug. "We've waited 'n' waited," Danny added, as if he were the twins' brother. He valiantly struggled down from his pony and received a hug.

"Run and tell the others we're coming," Joel ordered. The twins bounded to their horses, but Danny said, "A body's gotta help me. I can get down, not up." Boosted into the saddle, he turned his pony after the others and trotted off.

Smokey glanced at Cyrus Scott, whose hands toyed nervously with the reins. His Scott blue eyes stared at the ranch house visible from where they rested. Smokey turned away, struck to the core of his being. Although he knew the story, he could only guess at what the older man was experiencing. Slowly they started the descent to the Double J. Even Jim Perkins refrained from his joking. As they reached the corral, a group of people stood waiting. The shouting twins and Danny had done their heralding well. Smokey readily identified Gideon, the wronged brother, waiting for Cyrus with the flame of righteousness in his face. Judith, his faithful wife, stood beside him. How would she feel, seeing the man who long ago betrayed her sister?

A tall man and a slim, attractive woman next to him must be the Searses. No mistaking the older couple who stood rigid. Lige Scott bore a strong family resemblance to his sons and grandson. White-haired Naomi, with her proud carriage and aristocratic features, stood silently with brimming eyes.

Smokey hung back, filled with sudden bashfulness. But he could not tear his gaze from the scene. Joel leaped from Querida and strode to the lead wagon and waited until Cyrus stepped down. "My father and I are home," he said.

Without a moment's hesitation, Gideon limped forward and grabbed Cyrus. "Thank God you live!" Still-graceful Naomi came next, and Smokey looked away, unable to bear the sight of her face. He took a few steps back, intending to slip away. The mighty roll of a thunderous voice stopped everyone in their tracks.

"My son, my son." Lige came into his own. He plowed through the others, little heeding their presence until he stood face-to-face with Cyrus. "Can you ever forgive me?"

"*I,* forgive *you?*" Cyrus Scott dropped to the dusty ground and bowed his head before his father. With strength surprising in one so gaunt, Lige lifted his son and clasped him to his bosom as the prophets of old must have done. "You live. That is all that matters."

Smokey could stand no more. He backed away, mumbling that he'd see to the stock, and made his escape. He found things to do until Joel called him to meet the family. Then he managed to produce enough calm to cover his deep feelings and later went back to the corral where riders had come in from their day's duties.

The quartet of dusty cowhands said they answered to Lonesome, Dusty, Cheyenne, and Kansas. A keen-eyed older man who introduced himself as Fred Aldrich, foreman, took Smokey in at a lightning glance and "reckoned he'd be right useful on the Double J." The newcomer knew, as far as the cowboys were concerned, that remained to be seen. Smokey had ridden for enough outfits to recognize the need to prove himself before the longer-term hands accepted him. He grinned. No slouch at riding, roping, and shooting, he anticipated some fun.

Lights burned in the big ranch house until the early morning hours, but the cozy little cabin the Scotts had delighted in fixing up for Jim and Conchita went dark early. Given a choice of beds in the bunkhouse or a cabin of their own, Smokey and Curly chose the latter. "Although I ain't promising to stay with you any longer than it takes to get a yes out of a certain cook," Curly warned. A gleam in his eye added that his days as a cabinmate were already numbered.

The next day all the hands except those with the herd received a summons to a meeting. Gideon took charge, happiness exuding from every pore. "With all our new friends, we'll need to make some changes," he said simply. "We have the best cook in any Arizona bunkhouse, but with more to feed, Curly can prove invaluable. Mrs. Cook wants to help our housekeeper for a time." He grinned, and the worthy woman actually blushed.

"Smokey and Jim are no strangers to range work, and neither is Cyrus, as soon as he feels up to helping; Dad already is. Mom and Judith and Rebecca can do whatever no one else does." He paused. "Oh, we'll keep on all hands over the winter who want to help build some houses. This place is big enough for now, but by spring, Joel and Rebecca will need their own place."

Curly spoke up like a man. "So will I. Mrs. Cook is going to change her name right soon."

A round of applause greeted the statement followed by congratulations. Smokey slipped away as soon as he could without attracting attention. "More of the two by twos, doggone it," he complained good-naturedly to no one. "Oh, well, I can always slope if it gets too mushy around these parts."

Later that day, Joel sought him out. "Did you mean what you said about wanting a vacation?"

"Sure. I'm hankering to see some more of

this country before I settle down chasing cows."

"Then why don't you go anytime? In a week or so, we'll start the fall roundup. I don't suppose you want to miss that."

"Who, me?" Smokey drawled. "Say, Boss, you think you can have a roundup without me? That's like having Thanksgiving with no turkey."

"Settled." Joel lightly punched his friend's arm, then his face clouded over as suddenly as Arizona storm clouds in a clear sky. "The ranchers around here are friendly; so are most of the merchants and people in Flag. If you get down into the Tonto, be careful. Zeke Stockton, whose men shot Gideon that time, lives there. So do a lot of dark-browed riders no one knows much about. Rumors of outlaw gangs float up here now and then. Don't go poking around too much down in the brakes. Those folks are clannish and don't take kindly to strangers. There are stills in the woods and polecats, four legged and two legged. Watch where and how you ride."

"Thanks for the sermon, Boss, but I reckon Arizona bad men can't be much worse than New Mexico ones."

Joel's sharp retort shocked him. "Don't count on it. Other parts of the Southwest are getting more settled, but Arizona's still pretty wild. The way Gideon tells it, a lot of men no longer welcome in Texas, New Mexico, and Colorado are heading this way." He cleared his throat. "Vaya con Dios, and hurry back home."

Three days later, a rueful Smokey told Buckskin, "I should have listened better about these doggoned brakes. I've never been so turned around since that square dance back in New Mexico." He slid from the saddle and led his horse along a dim trail that must go somewhere unless it petered out the way several others had. He came to a little fork in the path, peered ahead, and caught a glimpse of blue. Then the patch moved. "Good, some feller's up ahead, and we can find out where we are," he said. Buckskin pricked her ears and followed.

The distant patch vanished behind a thicket. Smokey headed toward it. An inner sense of danger warned him. He stepped off the path and held his hand over Buckskin's nose so she wouldn't whinny. A dark figure came into view, bent low and almost creeping forward, as if stalking something or someone.

Smokey felt himself jerk. The figure's stealthy moves meant only trouble for the blue-shirted man ahead. The cowpuncher threw Buckskin's reins down and whispered, "Stand." The stalker had disappeared into the thicket without even a rustle.

Fair play born of an honest soul propelled Smokey after the figure. Inch by inch he followed, then veered a bit to the left so he could see better. He drew in his breath with a hissing sound. A coarse man stood hunched forward, peering through the thick bushes that screened him. His mouth stretched in a leer. His eyes gleamed with excitement.

Smokey frowned. The man made no move to pull a gun; he must not be planning to ambush his quarry. Shifting his position, Smokey let his gaze travel in the direction the stalker looked. Black anger filled him. The blue had not been part of a shirt but a calico dress.

His eyes noted in one lightning glance the slender figure that loosened silvery fair hair until it swung free; the worn moccasins she kicked off; the gleam of a dammed pool; the white face when she half turned before reaching for the top button on her simple dress.

Black rage for any man low enough to spy on a girl launched Smokey forward with a bellow. He landed squarely on top of the crouched dark figure who had been too engrossed to hear his attacker. The element of surprise served him well against the heavier man, that and the intensity of his fury. He seized the spying man by the waist, wrestled with him, then thrust him through the bushes, straight toward the girl.

CHAPTER 7

"You sniveling skunk!" Smokey Travis
pushed the hulking lout into the open. With
a low cry, the girl leaped to one side. Her
defender rushed the spy across the narrow
strip of sand and, with a gigantic shove, sent
him flying into the pool.

"You lowdown, rotten excuse for a man,"
Smokey raged. "If I ever catch you spying
on a girl again, I'll beat the living daylights
out of you an' tell every rancher and hand
between here and Flagstaff why. Who are
you, anyway?"

Mouth rilled with water, the floundering
man couldn't answer. He tried to stand but
slipped and fell back with a splash.

The cowboy turned to the girl and doffed
his sombrero. "Begging your pardon, Miss."
His dark eyes twinkled, and his teeth shone
white in the tanned face beneath his disheveled dark hair. "Do you know this polecat?"

Color sped into her white face. Her eyes

shone like jewels, and Smokey gasped. He'd seen many girls but never one like her. Barefooted, her silvery hair flying, she resembled a shy woodland creature more than a damsel in distress. When she spoke, her voice showed breeding and culture, not what he would have expected from a girl in the Tonto wilds. "His name is Hadley. He's my stepfather's foreman."

The words barely left her lips before an enraged howl from the brook warned that the soaked spy had finally regained his balance. He sounded more animal than human as he splashed toward them, clawing for his low-slung gun.

Before he got the dripping revolver halfway out of the holster, he found himself staring into Smokey's pistol barrel, trained straight at his heart and held in a rock-steady hand.

"Pitch your gun back in the creek," Smokey ordered. "Not that it will fire," he added with a meaningful glance at the Colt. "Then hightail it out of here, an' don't come back. This part of the woods could prove a mite unhealthy for skunks."

Enraged, Hadley lifted his revolver, but instead of obeying, he threw it straight at the cowboy's grinning face and rushed to knock his enemy to the ground.

Nimbly, Smokey leaped aside, sheathed his gun with one hand, and followed it with a punch that sent Hadley sprawling in an ignominious heap. Blood spurted from his nose, and a stream of garbled curses came from his mouth.

Smokey grabbed him by the shirtfront and backhanded him across the face. "Shut your foul mouth, Hadley, if you don't want a pistol-whipping." He gestured menacingly toward his gun. "There's a lady present. If she weren't here, I'd tie you to a tree an' give you what you deserve." He shoved Hadley's chest until the victim fell back to the sand. "At that, it's more than you deserve. Now get up an' get out."

A baleful look on his face, Hadley tramped into the bushes. Smokey called after him, "Don't think you can hide along the trail, either. I'd purely love having a good reason to shoot a hole in you."

A crash followed by a series of diminishing footfalls showed the threat had born fruit, but the foreman had the last word. Safely hidden from sight but still in earshot, he called back, "Columbine Ames, I'll get even. Wait until yore daddy hears about this. He's goin' to be real int'r'sted to know yore a-meetin' a cowboy behind his back." A suggestive laugh preceded running steps.

Why hadn't he killed the yellow dog when he had the chance? Smokey sprang toward the crushed bushes, but the girl, faster than a doe in flight, intercepted him. "Let him go." Scorn flashed in her magnificent eyes. "He's not worth shooting." Her shapely hand rested on his sleeve.

"All right, but I won't promise what will happen if I run up against him again." Smokey's keen eyes saw how her face blanched, and he added hastily, "I probably won't." He laughed cheerily. "Joel Scott said Arizona was full of surprises, but I sure didn't know I'd run into a bad man an' meet a pretty girl before I'd been here a week." The frank admiration in his voice robbed it of any boldness, and after a moment, Columbine laughed.

"I'm glad you came." A rich blush painted her face. "I never dreamed anyone knew I came here to bathe."

"Men like Hadley have ways. Better pick some other place," he soberly told her. "I have a hunch this little event won't make him feel too kindly toward you. A feller never likes to get showed up before a girl, 'specially one he likes."

Her involuntary look of repulsion told him even more than her words when she said, "He's a nightmare."

133

"Why doesn't your daddy run him off?"

Great tears welled and darkened the blue eyes. "I — I can't tell you." She took a step back. Fear swallowed every bit of color in her face. "Thank you, Mr. —"

"Smokey. Smokey Travis."

Some of her natural dignity returned. She held out a slim hand, and he awkwardly took it for a moment. It lay soft in his, yet he'd bet his favorite saddle blanket strength rested in that hand. "You saved me from an unpleasant time, if not worse, although I don't think Hadley would actually hurt me. He's too afraid of Father." Contempt underlined every word.

"Can he make trouble for you, like he said?"

Her fair head drooped. "I hope not, but Zeke's awfully jealous and . . . I mean, Zeke Stockton. He's not really my father but my stepfather. He married Mother three years ago. She died last year."

Her voice went ragged, and Smokey had the feeling a river of tears lurked behind her shining eyes. He pieced together what information he had: A jealous stepfather, who was none other than Zeke Stockton, and a foreman who sneaked around watching her bathe made Columbine Ames's life no Sunday picnic.

A daring idea slipped into Smokey's brain. "A long time ago something happened an' my pards an' I up an' beat another crooked foreman to the boss. I told him the truth. Wail 'til I get Buckskin, an' I'll take you home. We'll tell your daddy — Zeke — what really happened."

Stark terror swept into her face. "No, oh, no! He'd kill you."

"Who? Hadley? Some chance. Come on, Miss Ames. It's the only way to clear you."

Hope struggled with fear and won, but she still sounded doubtful. "All right. I just don't want killing because of me."

"Some men need killing, don't they?"

"Only God can judge that," she told him quietly. "Promise me that no matter what happens, you won't pull a gun."

He reached for his discarded sombrero and smiled at her. "I won't unless it's to save my life or yours." He saw his words didn't fully satisfy her, so he continued. "Aw, nothing like that's going to happen. Hadley's yellow clear through. He's more likely to dry gulch a man than stand up an' face him."

All the way to the Cross Z ranch house, Smokey kept up a patter of conversation designed to relieve her mind. Twice he succeeded in making her laugh and thrilled to

135

the sound. Long before they halted out of sight of the prosperous ranch buildings, Smokey suspected why he'd come to Arizona.

As Columbine dismounted, a man appeared from nowhere and stepped around a bend in the road. Smokey reached for his gun. "Who're you, an' what do you want?" he barked.

Brown eyes widened beneath a shock of corn-colored hair. The youth's hands shot into the air. "Columbine, are you all right?"

Something in the question caused Smokey to lower his gun. "Andy, this is Smokey Travis. He caught Hadley spying on me," Columbine inserted quickly. She cast an imploring glance at her rescuer. Smokey realized she didn't want to go into any details and nodded slightly. The lithe rider who looked about her age had stiffened at the foreman's name. Hot color poured into his cheeks.

"Put her there," he said and gripped Smokey's hand. The cowboy returned the grip. Something flashed between them, and he felt better about the situation. Unless he were dead wrong, Columbine Ames had a young but true-blue friend in Andy.

"We're riding in so Stockton can learn the truth," Smokey told the other.

136

"Too late. Hadley's beat you to it."

"Then we'll just have to convince him different." Smokey didn't give them time to protest but coolly marched ahead and around the bend. The house loomed before them. So did a group of hawk-faced riders. No open-faced cowboys here, bent on devilment but basically decent. Smokey thought of Joel's warning about the brakes.

Clannish . . . don't take kindly to strangers . . . a lot of men no longer welcome in Texas and New Mexico and Colorado are heading this way . . . Arizona is still pretty wild.

He could believe it from the looks of the bunch ahead, some lounging against the corral, others astride dark horses. "Which one's Stockton? I don't see Hadley."

His answer came in the form of a door slammed open so hard its bang resounded in the tense, waiting air. A man catapulted from the house. Smokey sized him up in a glance. Six feet, close to two hundred pounds, sandy hair, colorless eyes now blazing hatred and something unreadable. He flung himself across the porch, closely followed by Hadley, whose expression of triumph changed ludicrously when Smokey stepped into his line of vision.

Never one to let another get the drop on

him, Smokey halted Stockton's impetuous rush toward Columbine with a clear, ringing call. "Hadley, how'd you have the guts to come back here after I caught you spying on Miss Ames at her bathing place?"

"What's that?" Like a tormented bull, the rancher whirled around. "Who the devil are you, and what are you doing here?" Understanding crept into his fury-driven brain. "Say, are you the puncher Hadley told me about?"

"Ump-umm. I'm the one he lied about." Smokey sprang forward. "I never saw your daughter before in my life, Stockton. I did some fishing, got turned around in the brakes, an' run across your foreman peeking through the bushes. He never saw anything. I got him just when Miss Ames had kicked off her moccasins." Truth rang white-hot in his voice.

"It's a lie, it's a lie," Hadley raved. Foam appeared at the corner of his mouth, and his eyes rolled. He reached for his gun and swore when his fingers touched the empty holster. "This cowboy jumped me 'cause I saw him following Colley."

"You told me they were meeting," Stockton roared, his great hands clenching and unclenching.

"I mighta been wrong," he mumbled.

138

Streams of sweat ran down his dark face.

"He's a liar, Father." The bell-like voice turned the players in the scene to statues. Columbine stepped forward. "It happened just the way Mr. Travis said."

Smokey's heart nearly burst with pride. All the girl's earlier nervousness had fled. She stood straight and fearless, facing her enemies, as if protected by an unseen force.

"You —" Stockton snatched for his gun. Hadley's life hung in the balance.

"Hold it!" Smokey drew his gun so fast, a ripple of shock ran through the onlookers.

The rancher's half-raised revolver froze in midair. "Keep out of it, Travis," he roared.

Smokey didn't budge. "You want to kill a man right here before *your daughter?*" he ground out, instinctively hitting Stockton's weak spot.

The big man quivered. With a mighty backhand swing, he knocked Hadley senseless with the hand still holding the gun. "Haul him off the ranch, and tell him if I ever see him again, I'll shoot on sight." Raving, he glared at Smokey. "You ride out, too. If I owe you thanks, this will settle it." He pulled a fistful of bills from his shirt pocket and flung them on the ground in front of the cowboy.

"Father, how could you, after what he

did?" Columbine's eyes became grief-filled gulfs; her face went hot with shame.

"Go to your room and stay there," he ordered.

She obeyed but only after saying in a voice that reached every person there, "At least I am grateful."

Smokey tipped his sombrero, kicked the money out of his way, and mounted Buckskin. "Glad to oblige. Adiós, Miss Ames, Stockton." He nodded at the others and winked at Andy, then touched his heels to the mare. But he couldn't resist hollering at the top of his lungs when she leaped and settled into a steady stride, "Yippee-ay!"

A quarter mile down the road, Smokey reined in and hid Buckskin in a cottonwood grove. His senses alert to possible pursuit, he wormed his way back and gained a vantage point from which he had a wide view of the ranch house, corral, and bunkhouse. Columbine and Stockton had vanished. Two disgusted-looking men busily loaded Hadley's limp form into a wagon. Young Andy stood by the corral gazing up at a window Smokey knew must be Columbine's. His hard, young face told its own story.

On impulse, Smokey worked closer, until his low call would reach the lad but not the others. "Andy," he hissed. "Don't turn. It's Smokey."

A convulsive jerk was the only sign the cowboy had heard.

"Start whistling, then kind of easylike walk to the cottonwoods," Smokey directed. He grunted with satisfaction at the nonchalant way Andy carried out his orders. He waited fifteen full minutes, then slithered back the way he'd come.

A white-faced rider stepped from the grove. "Mr. Travis, I —"

"Smokey."

Andy gulped. "Smokey. I 'most choked when you called Hadley." Admiration shone clear and bright in his brown eyes.

Playing on a hunch, Smokey demanded, "Why are you working for Stockton and his rustlers?" He planted his hands on his hips. The reply would help him take measure of the boy's manhood.

He wasn't disappointed. Andy offered neither an apology nor a stammering denial of the charge. "God an' me are the only friends Columbine Ames has. I've stood a lot to stay here for her sake."

"Are you in love with her?"

"I used to be." The steady gaze never wavered. "Who could help loving a girl like her?"

141

"And now?"

Seriousness gave way to fun. "Naw, I'm her friend. She needs that a heap more than a moonstruck hand her daddy-who-ain't would fire off the place in a minute. I've got another girl. How about you?"

Smokey roared and clapped him on the shoulder. "Never had much time for girls, but I'll be hanged if I've ever seen one like her."

"She's just as sweet and good inside as out," Andy told him. "Her ma taught her the Bible, and if anyone lives it, why, that's got to be Columbine. She tried to make me promise I wouldn't ever shoot anyone, even a two-legged skunk. Says killing's plumb wrong and against everything God intended." His eyes slitted. "I didn't promise, though. If anyone ever lays a hand on her, I'll kill him."

"Can she shoot? Does she have a gun?"

"Yeah and yeah." Andy lowered his voice and repeated the story of Columbine's stay in the cave after her stepfather frightened her. "I made her keep my pistol and got me another one." He sighed, and his shoulders fell dejectedly. "I'm not sure she'd use it, though."

"Then we have to get her away from here."

Andy didn't act surprised that the stranger

had pinpointed exactly what he'd decided weeks earlier. "We used to talk, but lately I can't get near her. Trouble is, she won't be eighteen 'til next July."

Smokey pondered. "Since Stockton's no blood kin, by law he has no right to keep her here against her will."

Andy snorted. "Law! In the Tonto? Man, if we had a sheriff, which we don't most of the time 'cept for one that meanders out here from Payson or Pine now and then, more 'n likely he'd be in for his cut." He raised an eyebrow. "How come I'm telling you all this, anyway? Who knows but what you're another Billy the Kid."

"I might be, but I'm not. Besides, look what happened to him," Smokey. reminded. "Shot and killed before he was twenty-three. I don't figure on that happening to me." *Especially now,* he mentally added.

"Shh," Andy warned, crouching low. The *clip-clop* of hooves on the road and the sound of voices stilled them until the wagon with Hadley had moved out of sight.

"So what can be proved against Stockton?" Smokey didn't want to waste any time.

"Not a thing so far." Andy grimaced, and a lock of his bright hair fell over his forehead. "I suspect the big roundup he's planning will be the last. He hinted as much to

Columbine, said he'd gotten tired of Arizona. I ain't supposed to know this, but I listen real good in the bunkhouse when I'm snoring the loudest." A likable grin lit up his face. "The men are uneasy, wondering what's going to happen, so Stockton ain't told them everything. Say, who're you riding for?"

"The Double J."

Andy let out a whistle. "That's where I aimed to go looking for a job after I found out there's a lot of shady goings-on down here. Then Columbine needed me."

"There will always be a job on the Double J any time you want it," Smokey assured him. "If we could get Miss Ames there, the Scotts would take her in."

"I figured she could probably get on clerking at Babbitt's in Flag," Andy put in.

"I'm not sure she'd be safe there. She would be at the ranch." A look of complete understanding passed between them, then Andy reluctantly stood.

"I'd better get back. Stockton's suspicious of everyone these days." He cocked his head and grinned. "It would be a fine thing if an upstanding cowboy who doesn't drink or smoke or hang around saloons and loose women fell in love with Columbine and her with him. Of course, he'd have to figure out how to kidnap her and marry her without Zeke knowing it."

Smokey felt red creep under his skin, but he blandly agreed. "A fine thing. If I meet a feller like that, I'll tell him to keep it in mind."

Andy haw-hawed and slipped away. Smokey thoughtfully retrieved Buckskin, who stood grazing nearby, and headed northwest, forgetting that he'd planned to fish some more. Now all he wanted was to get to the Double J and figure out what to do about a slip of a girl with big blue eyes and a flower face who bloomed pure and innocent in the blackest of surroundings.

When he came to the trampled grass and bushes that led to the little pool where he first saw her, Smokey couldn't resist turning out of his way to visit the spot again. How had he missed the beauty of the glade, the shining water in the early evening hush, the white sand and whispering cottonwoods? "Whoa," he told Buckskin and slid from the saddle. He retraced his steps. Here he had seen Hadley, evil all over his face. Fresh rage washed over him, but he shoved it aside and walked into the clearing. His face stared back at him from the still pool. Black eyes blazed; black hair crept from beneath his sombrero. A grim line to his jaw dissolved in a reluctant smile. "If I looked like that when I came bursting from the bushes, it's a wonder she didn't run from Hadley *an'* me," he told his watery image.

A few minutes later, he went back to his horse, wondering why the secluded spot seemed hallowed by the girl's presence, and something more. A sleepy birdsong followed him, the whirr of wings. Unwilling to break the pensive mood that had overtaken him, Smokey rode slowly until he found a good spot to make camp.

After a frugal meal from the supplies he carried in his saddlebags, he stretched out with his head on his saddle, a blanket around him. Great white stars smiled down, mysterious and knowing. A gentle wind rose and crooned through the trees. More keenly than ever before, Smokey realized how right Joel had been. *Arizona did have a music of its own: of good and evil, happiness and danger, beauty and ugliness. But most of all, of love.*

CHAPTER 8

"Boss, can I talk to you?"

Joel Scott looked up from the bridle he was mending. "Sure, Smokey. What's on your mind?" Dead serious, Smokey lounged against the barn door, his face somber. His tanned cheeks flushed slightly, but his gaze remained steady.

"Do you believe in love at first sight?"

Joel gasped and dropped the bridle. Never in a thousand years would he have expected such a question. "Why . . ." His face showed shock.

"The first time you saw Rebecca Fairfax, did you feel kinda warm inside, that you'd do anything to protect her?" Smokey anxiously waited for the answer. Since he had returned from the Tonto Basin, a fair-haired girl's flower face and blue eyes seldom left his thoughts. Neither did the anger that she lived in a nest of vipers. Cautiously, he had sounded out the hands in the bunkhouse without telling them why. Lonesome, Dusty, Kansas, and Cheyenne all declaimed Zeke Stockton vehemently. As Lonesome put it, his show of respectability "doesn't fool no one."

Foreman Fred Aldrich, who kept the Double J outfit on the straight and narrow, added sourly, "He's pure mean and poison underneath but smoother than cream when he takes the notion."

The peril surrounding Columbine Ames was real, Smokey reflected soberly as he listened eagerly to Joel's reply. The young cowboy minister's eyes glowed like the Arizona sky at its bluest.

"You've hit it square, Pard. And every time I saw her after that, it got worse."

"Ah-uh. That's what I figured."

"Once I knew she cared, too, I felt God had led me to New Mexico so I could not only find my father but meet her and save her from Hayes." Remembrance crept into his face. "It's all I can do to wait a few more weeks until we marry." His expression changed. "Womenfolk need more time to get ready, I guess, but I'm glad we waited until we could be with the whole family." He let out a cowboy yell that startled the horses in the corral and set them to dancing. The next instant, he quietly asked,

"Who is she?"

"Who is who?" But Smokey knew his face gave him away.

"The Arizona girl you want to protect." Joel wasn't to be sidetracked.

Smokey gave up all pretense of merely asking for information of the heart. "I ran across a mess down in the Tonto." He described his recent adventure in a few terse sentences. "Columbine Ames looks just like the flower, kinda frail an' delicate. She's not, though. You should have seen her stand up to Zeke Stockton, 'her daddy-who-ain't,' Andy Cullen calls him."

"Who's Andy Cullen?" Joel demanded. "I already know — too well — who Stockton is." The corners of his mouth turned down.

"A shock-haired kid, maybe eighteen. Corn-colored hair, big brown eyes that don't miss much, an' according to him, Columbine's only friend, except God." Smokey noticed how his friend's face lit up, as if someone had set a fire behind his eyes.

"If she knows God, she has a protector," Joel reminded.

"Sure, but doggone it, I hate to think there's no one looking after her here on earth except Andy. He's a hothead, an' sooner or later, Stockton will get wise to him an' boot him off the Cross Z. What'll

149

she do then?"

A little pool of silence fell between them, the silence of range men comfortable with one another. Then Smokey added, "I've seen lots of pretty faces an' lots of good girls, but I never saw one whose eyes are so innocent. You know she's the real thing all the way through. Andy said her ma taught her from the Bible." He shifted his weight and dug the toe of one boot into the dusty ground. "There's something about her that makes a man, if he *is* a man, want to take care of her."

"Is that all?"

Smokey shook his head and looked without fear into his boss's sympathetic face. "Before you rode up to the Lazy F, I never thought no girl or woman could beat Rebecca." He raised his head and watched a hawk sail by. It reminded him of the predatory look in Hadley's face. "I always knew, though, I wasn't the one for her, 'specially when you came. I still think she's pretty close to one of those angels you talk about, an' I'm proud to be her friend all this time." His clear eyes held frank pride.

"I appreciate your honesty," Joel told him.

"Somehow, it's different with Columbine. Don't say anything to Perkins. He's a true an' faithful pard, but he talks too much, an'

I don't feel like being joshed. She might never even look at a cowpoke like me. She sure won't if her stepdaddy has his say." Smokey's face darkened, and his hands clenched. "Stockton about went crazy when his wife died, an' Columbine's the picture of her mother, according to Andy. He thinks Stockton's got them kind of confused in his mind. Anyway, he's bound to marry her with or without her say-so."

"And you aim to stop him."

"I do." Smokey's eyes glittered, and he straightened. "Boss, what I want to know is, are you with me? You saved my life, an we've been comrades ever since. If somehow Andy an' I can smuggle her here, will you back me?"

"With all my heart." Joel's hand shot out, and Smokey gripped it, feeling the depth of commitment in the clasp. "Stockton has no legal claim on the girl. If she needs a place to stay, Judith and Rebecca and everyone else here on the ranch will make her welcome." His eyes sparkled. "At least until you convince her that Columbine Travis is a better handle than Columbine Ames."

Smokey's grip tightened at the idea, and his heart pounded. "An' if necessary, you'll fight for her?"

A shadow clouded Joel's blue eyes. "We'll

151

pray God uses a different way, but yes, we'll fight for her. If she's as sweet as you say, every man on the Double J will defend her."

All during the fall roundup, Smokey went through the physical motions while his mind was far away. Every time he saw Conchita waiting on the little cabin porch for Jim, he smiled and saw himself riding in to find Columbine standing on a similar porch, her blue dress fluttering. Sometimes he called himself loco, but the dreams persisted. They intensified as the day grew closer for Joel and Rebecca's wedding. They'd chosen to keep it simple, with only family and the outfit present. Once when Smokey reported in from the range, he saw Rebecca's bright brown head bent over some frothy white stuff that looked like a waterfall. The happiness in her brown eyes when she looked up brought a smile to his lips. Perhaps someday . . .

Curly and Mrs. Cook had already tied the knot. He drove her into Flag, ostensibly to order supplies. She came back wearing a store-bought dark blue dress with white frill at the neck and a brand-new wedding ring! "We didn't want to take the shine off your and Becky's wedding," the new bride told Joel and Rebecca. "Figured this was best." She cast a proud look at Curly, resplendent in a new cowboy outfit complete with bright scarf and Stetson. "We'd have liked for you to hitch us, but I reckon we're just as married this way."

That night a loud singing rang around the cabin hastily vacated by Smokey. He moved into the bunkhouse with the rest of the Double J hands, all of whom had long since been foiled in their tricks and now accepted him as one of them. His cheerful attitude and willingness to do more than his fair share of the hard work had been his initiation to the ranch.

Smokey also had hours to consider his growing feelings concerning the Scripture Joel used when he preached every Sabbath afternoon. No one on the Double J listened more carefully than the New Mexico cowhand. Not one of the townspeople who faithfully drove out for services realized that in the rough-hewn cowboy's innermost places, the cry for God gradually grew to a shout.

One crisp afternoon astride Buckskin, Smokey opened up to God. "I can see a feller needs the Almighty, but, God, if You're the Trailmate Joel and Gideon say You are, how come You made rattlesnakes like Zeke Stockton?"

Buckskin had no answer, and Smokey

rode on, torn between conviction and his determination to serve Columbine. How could he invite the Lord into a heart bent on freeing her from bondage, no matter what the cost?

At last the roundup ended with the herd bunched and ready to drive to the market. As soon as they'd been sold and the cowboys came home, Joel and Rebecca would marry. Smokey began to breathe easier. No more had been heard of Stockton and his crooked dealings or of Hadley. Then Jim Perkins rode in, wearing a bloody bandage and madder than a wet cat. He tumbled off his sorrel mare, blazing eyes showing he hadn't been fatally wounded, and clumped to the bunkhouse porch. "Half the herd's been stolen," he blurted out. "Saddle up." He reeled and would have fallen if Smokey hadn't leaped forward and caught him. He lowered Jim to his own bunk. "Go get Conchita, someone," he barked.

"No," Jim hollered. "It'll scare her to death. Get some of the blood off me first."

"Hey, Aldrich," Lonesome sang out when the foreman appeared in the doorway to see what had caused the commotion. "Our herd's done gone astray with some help from rustlers."

He sprang into action. "Kansas, get Gid-

154

eon and Joel. Cheyenne, ride for Eb Sears. Good thing his cabin ain't far. Dusty, the rest of you, we're ridin' soon as you can get the horses saddled."

So it had come, the fight the Double J had expected. Smokey hastily removed the stained bandage from Perkins's head, but before he could bathe the slight groove, the women arrived and took over.

"Snappin' crocodiles, the first excitement since I reached Arizona, and here I am weaker'n a newborn foal!" Jim complained.

"Hush." Conchita pushed him back on the bunk. "They can get along without you."

"That's what I'm afeared of," he said comically. "Once the boys find out I ain't necessary, I'll be out of a job."

Smokey laughed along with the others, then hurried out. Buckskin stood saddled and waiting, courtesy of one of the hands. A quick leap into the saddle, a touch of boot heels to her sides, and she responded like the thoroughbred she was.

A long night followed, then a day and another night. The tracks led into the worst part of the brakes. Before the pursuers left the ranch, Jim had admitted he didn't know how long he'd been knocked out, so the rustlers could have had a head start. Yet the unshaven Double J riders kept on. Smokey

155

didn't voice his fear that this was Stockton's doing. He could be wrong. The supposedly honest rancher and his cohorts weren't the only outlaws in the Tonto. Yet from the start, a dozen comments floated to his ears about "Stockton's doings."

Once, a wild idea crossed his mind. This would be a perfect time to rescue Columbine. With Zeke busy elsewhere, Smokey could spirit her away. Yet for better or for what would certainly be worse, his loyalty to the outfit prevented desertion even for a worthy cause.

By late afternoon, they knew they were closing in. Riders outstripped moving cattle even when constrained by the need for caution. Ahead lay a box canyon Aldrich pronounced ideal for rustled cattle: water, plenty of grass, and no way out once they were inside. "Dismount, and don't show yourselves," he ordered. "Duck from the thickets to behind trees and keep low. There's bound to be lookouts. They'll know we had more than one night guard."

Dread filled Smokey at what lay before them. Why did the God Joel preached about let wicked men despoil this beautiful country? Would some of the Double J outfit be killed in the fight?

Grazing cattle filled the canyon. Yellow

leaves turned in the breeze and fell. Dark pines and cedar contrasted with the golden world.

"All right, rustlers. We've got enough men to keep you holed in until Judgment Day," Aldrich bawled. His voice echoed against the rock walls of the canyon. "This is Aldrich, Double J."

A string of curses followed, splintering the mountain air. "Come 'n' git us."

"We don't have to," Lonesome yelled.

Have to, have to, came the echo.

"We'll just stick out here 'til you starve," Dusty bellowed, and again it echoed.

Coarse laughter followed. Aldrich and his men pulled back into the mouth of the canyon and made camp out of rifle shot. Smokey pondered the situation and walked to Joel, who stared at the herd with misery in his face. "Think there has to be killing?"

"I hope not. I'm sworn not to kill, but I can't let our outfit be gunned down, and we can't just let rustlers steal our cattle." His still-boyish face looked sick.

"I have an idea that might work. Wait until dark an' let me get the lay of the land," Smokey whispered. The moment dusk fell, he slipped away, worked clear around the herd, and came back grinning. "We can do it an' never fire a shot," he gleefully told the outfit who gathered around him. "Here's my plan. There's no cabin; the rustlers are camped at the far end of the canyon. Only three men are guarding the herd 'cause they can't go anywhere except this way. Now what we do is . . ." He laid it out nice and sweet. "Aldrich, what do you say? Boss? Sears?"

All nodded, and Lonesome burst out admiringly, "Say, you're a smart cuss."

"I will be if it works," Smokey reminded him as he settled his sombrero more firmly on his head. "Remember, don't make any noise until I holler."

"Then all everything's gonna break loose," one of the cowboys chimed in.

"We hope." Smokey raised his hand and crossed his fingers. "I'll give you fifteen minutes to get in your places."

He disappeared back into the welcome darkness. The moon had obligingly stayed behind a ridge, and a few clouds hid some of the stars. Smokey again skirted the herd to the opposite side, noting with satisfaction the way they had bunched together for the night. "All right, Buckskin," he commanded in a low voice. "Yippee-ay!" His shout rang sudden and clear, magnified by the echoes in the canyons and returned by the band of Double J cowboys. Smokey followed it up by shooting in the air and riding straight into the herd.

The pandemonium caused by the echoes spooked the herd. First they milled, then ably assisted by the Double J rider bent low in the saddle, the cattle began to run toward the mouth of the canyon. "Whoopee!" Smokey roared and followed, shooting until his revolver emptied, then reloading while he rode. He could hear Aldrich bellowing orders from one side, Joel on the other. A volley of shots from the upper end of the canyon harmlessly whistled past, and Smokey laughed jubilantly. Yet when his comrades had driven the herd out of the canyon and toward the distant Double J, he couldn't resist the temptation to tether Buckskin at a safe distance and creep back to the rustlers' fire. Like a snake, he slithered on his belly to a lookout behind a small pile of rock that had fallen from the canyon walls.

Carefully he raised his head and froze. *Hadley!* He scanned the other faces, many bearded, all dark and sullen. Relief shot through him. Stockton wasn't among them.

Footfalls a little to his right made him drop his face until the sombrero hid the gleam of moonlight on his cheeks. Three more angry men had joined the little band by the small fire.

"Where in the name of all that's holy were you?" Hadley raged, his face livid in the firelight. A scar on one side of his face, evidently from Stockton's gun, showed clearly. "Fine bunch you are. Let the Double J ride out of here with a herd yore supposed to be guardin'."

"You couldn't a-done no better," one flared. Smokey recognized him as a Cross Z man, one of those by the corral the day he took Columbine home. A little thrill went through him.

"Yore loco. I never shoulda took you on when I split with Stockton," Hadley snapped.

"Quit bellyachin', Hadley," someone called. Smokey turned toward the voice. A dark figure had thrown a saddle over a horse and stood pulling the girth tight. He swung aboard. "The Double J outfit's gonna be back here as soon as they get the herd settled down. I'm ridin' out before they come. This deal stinks like a dead skunk. I wasn't above double-crossin' Stockton, but I ain't aimin' to get killed, 'specially now there's no cattle deal." He spurred his horse and disappeared in the darkness.

Hadley swore and pulled his gun, but a hand next to him knocked it upward before he could pull the trigger. "No use wastin' bullets. He's right. Let's scatter and meet somewheres healthier." A murmur of assent ran through the band of men.

Hadley lowered his voice and gestured, and the men nodded. "Slip past while they're still settlin' the herd," their leader called. "No sense gettin' yoreselves killed. Nobody seen us, so they can't prove nothin'."

Oh, yeah? Smokey grinned in the shadows. *Well, Mr. Rustler Hadley, you're wrong about that. Dead wrong.* His grin faded. This time there had been no killing, but what about the next time? And the next? Soberly, Smokey rejoined his outfit and told them the outlaws had sneaked off. Privately, he wondered why he felt so glad Zeke Stockton had not been part of the raid.

Shortly after reaching the ranch, the cowboys collected the rest of the cattle earmarked for sale and made their drive. "The ones that got stolen dropped a bit in weight," he told Joel. "But that's just so many more that won't be stolen over the winter when they drift down into the draws."

"Right, and we avoided a shoot-out." Joel beamed.

"That's 'cause I wasn't there," Perkins

told them. He cocked one eyebrow and flashed the cherubic smile he used on occasion to infuriate his pards.

"At least we're not letting any little old no-'count hurt keep us from working," Smokey told him sarcastically.

"Connie says I can't ride 'til it's healed." Jim smirked. "She's afraid I might get blood poisonin' or sunstroke or —"

Smokey cut off his list of possible maladies by snorting loudly. As he walked off with Joel, he couldn't help grinning at his boss. "Jim's never going to get over missing our raid."

Joel sighed. "I'm afraid there will be more." He shrugged. "Winter should be quiet except for the sound of hammering. There's plenty of room in the ranch house, but I can't wait for Rebecca and me to have our own home."

Days later, the golden-haired man and pretty Rebecca in her white gown stood before Gideon and pledged their love and lives to one another. She looked more like an angel than ever to Smokey, but, to Smokey's amazement, when she lifted her face toward her new husband, her features changed. Silvery fair hair replaced nut-brown. Radiant blue eyes shone instead of merry brown.

He drew in a quick breath. Could a man ask for more in life than Joel now had: a share in a ranch, a charming companion-wife, a God whose presence never faltered? No matter what storms came, the two who had promised to become one could stand.

Words from months earlier came into his mind . . . *after the fire a still small voice*. Joel and Rebecca knew that voice and heeded it. So did Gideon and Judith, Eb and Lily Sears, Lige and Naomi, and even Cyrus Scott, who had ignored it for long years. An unspoken prayer rose in Smokey's heart. *Please . . .* But he couldn't go on. Too many things crowded it out as the wind and the earthquake and the fire had in the Bible story. Smokey sighed. Would he ever come to terms with life and God? The minor strain in the music of the Arizona mountains so often foreshadowed joy. As if on cue, the next day Andy Cullen arrived at the Double J.

CHAPTER 9

A wide grin lit up Andy Cullen's likable face and set his mischievous brown eyes twinkling. "Howdy." He slid from the saddle of the nondescript horse carrying the Z brand and strode toward Smokey. "What's the chances of a bed and some of that Southern hospitality the Double J's famous for?"

Smokey leaped from his seat on the top bunkhouse step where he'd been waiting for Curly to beat the supper gong. "You're a sight for sore eyes," he told the younger rider. "All duded up, too." His quick gaze took in new jeans, checked shirt, and bright neckerchief. "How'd you get out of jail?"

Andy's grin faded. "It ain't jail for me but —" He lowered his voice and mysteriously nodded his head toward the corral.

Smokey got the message. Together they strolled to the privacy of the corral, empty except for horses. Tired riders had finished their day's work and headed for soap and water before the supper call.

"Is everyone all right at the ranch?" Smokey held his breath.

Andy's steady gaze never wavered. "Sure, if you think being penned up's all right." He then burst out indignantly, "Ever since that business with Hadley, Stockton's been a bear. I don't know how much longer I can hang on. Only reason I got away was 'cause of a sore tooth that needed pulling, so I came to Flag." He gingerly patted his jaw, and Smokey saw the slight swelling.

Andy went on. "Columbine's getting real pale and thin, not that she's ever been what anyone would call real sturdy except inside. A couple of times we got a minute to chat. She doesn't know what to make of Zeke." Andy pulled off his sombrero and tousled his already messed-up shock of hair. "Says he's leaving her strictly alone. I guess he hasn't mentioned you or Hadley or anything except she's not to get out of sight of the ranch house." Andy snorted inelegantly. "It's pitiful. Columbine's always loved the woods and to run free and wild. Once I saw a squirrel a feller had in a cage. It just went round and round. I waited 'til the man's back was turned, then just happened to lurch against the cage. The latch jarred loose. The squirrel took off and never came back."

Smokey caught the significance of the story. He sighed, his dark eyes troubled. "Sounds like Miss Ames needs someone to get her loose, that is, accidentally."

"Just before I rode out, I made so bold as to holler, 'Miss Columbine, you need anything from Flag?' Zeke clouded up like a summer storm, but all his scowling didn't faze her.

" 'Why, thanks, Cullen,' sez she. Zeke hates it if she calls the men by first names. Anyway, she asked me to wait for a minute while she made a list. Her eyes got all shiny, and she said, 'I need white thread and some buttons; I'll give you one to match.'

" 'I ain't in no hurry,' I told her, not being eager to get a tooth pulled. Stockton didn't budge, so I settled more comfortable in the saddle until she came out and give me an envelope." His eyes gleamed. "Funny thing. When I got to Flag and pulled it out, I found a list, a button, and this." He held out another envelope, creased from being folded into a tiny packet.

"What . . ." Smokey stared. Blood rushed to his clear, tanned skin. *Mr. Smokey Travis* in steady handwriting adorned the envelope.

"That's what I thought," Andy explained

cheerfully. "When it took longer than I figured at the doctor's — he ain't much better than a horse doctor — why, it got too late to start back today." His voice hardened. "Besides, Columbine Ames gave me a letter to deliver 'cause she trusted me. I didn't want to pass it on to just anybody."

"Thanks, Andy." Smokey still couldn't believe he actually held a message from the girl whose face haunted him.

"Reckon I'll go get some of the trail dust off me," Andy considerately told him and walked back toward the bunkhouse.

Gratitude for the plucky young man's loyalty filled Smokey. He glanced both ways to make sure no one observed him, then took the further precaution of slowly wandering to the shade of a nearby aspen. The greenish-white trunk showed naked now that most of the golden leaves had fallen. He tore open the envelope, noting the lack of any attempt at sealing.

Dear Mr. Travis — Smokey,
I apologize for Father's rudeness. He can be pleasant but lately appears to have a lot on his mind.
Perhaps someday I will see you again. Your actions and chivalry told me you would be a good friend, if circumstances

were different. God bless you.

Instead of a signature, a tiny sketch showed a delicate Rocky Mountain columbine waving in a breeze.

If he hadn't adored her already, the brief note would have sealed his infatuation. The words blurred. He, Smokey Travis, considered chivalrous by a girl trapped in the Tonto Basin! He read the message again, rejoicing that it had come, then stuffed it inside his shirt, where it lay close to his heart. Wearing a range-weary look as a mask, he answered the summons for supper when it came.

Known for an open welcome for any drifting cowpuncher who needed bed and board, the Double J saw nothing unusual about Andy's visit. Lonesome plied him with questions about fish in the creeks. Dusty reckoned he'd go catch one soon as the ranch could spare him. The other boys alternately joshed and heckled the visitor.

Smokey barely controlled the urge to knock his comrades' heads together. He wanted to talk with Andy alone. Knowing Smokey's intentions, the young man yawned and stood.

"Me for a little fresh air before hitting the sack. Smokey, you want any?"

"Might as well." Leisurely, he followed Andy out.

"If you happen to want to send an answer, I could smuggle it in to her with the thread and buttons," the go-between tempted.

Smokey's heart bounced. "Are you sure she's safe with Stockton?" he whispered.

"For now."

The sound of steps and Lonesome's plaintive, "I gotta roll out early. Wish a coupla galoots would get in here so we c'n blow out the lamp," ended the conversation.

The next morning, Smokey volunteered to check on a fence in the direction Andy had to take. Out of sight of the ranch, he fumbled in his jacket pocket for pencil and paper and dashed off a quick note. "Here, give her this. An' if she ever needs me, send word."

"I will." The note vanished under the string of a small, brown-paper package before Andy shoved it in his shirt. Moments later, he galloped off, leaving Smokey to watch him out of sight. How he wished he could be the one heading toward the Cross Z and Columbine!

He mulled over Andy's dubious assurance that, at least for the present, Zeke offered no threat. What of the upcoming winter months, months filled with idle hours?

Smokey shivered. If only he had a way to get Columbine to the Double J. If he rode in, Stockton would throw him out. If he enlisted Andy's aid in abduction, the boy would be fired if discovered, no matter how willing the victim was to go. Then Columbine would have to stand off her stepfather alone. Smokey couldn't take the risk.

There on the range, with Buckskin standing quietly beneath him, Smokey bared his head and looked toward heaven. "I don't know You very well, but she does. She trusts an' believes in You. Don't let her down." After a few seconds, he crammed the hat back on his dark hair and goaded the mare into a dead run.

When Zeke Stockton dismissed Smokey ungraciously, Columbine had fled for the safety of her room. Screened by her window curtain, she watched the rest of the drama. Her keen eyes observed the disdainful way the young man kicked the money Stockton had flung at him out of the way. She heard the farewell, "Adiós," in the clear, carrying voice followed by the wild, "Yippee-ay!"

Her heart thundered in her chest, but she never took her fascinated gaze from the scene. She caught Andy looking up toward her window, and then a slight movement of bushes a little behind the cowboy alerted her senses. "He must have slipped back," she murmured. Fear attacked her. "Please, God, don't let him get caught." There had been one near-killing today. If Smokey returned, tragedy might result.

Heavy footsteps in the hall froze her in place.

"Colley?" A light rap on the door brought her upright and away from the window. She leaped to her bed and called, "Come in."

Zeke opened the door and stepped inside, his large frame almost filling the doorway. "I want the truth. Have you been meeting with Travis?"

"I have not. Everything happened just as he said." She proudly raised her head. "You know me; you shouldn't have to ask such a question."

A subtle change softened the suspicion in his face. "How am I supposed to keep track of what you do?" The closest thing to an apology shone in his colorless eyes. "You're a good girl. Always have been. But you can't trust these drifters. None of them is any good, and they'll chase anything in skirts."

Columbine wanted to cry out in defense of the one who had saved her from embarrassment if not worse. But a look at Zeke's face halted the rush of words. "He isn't a

171

drifter," she instead offered meekly. "Smokey Travis came west with Joel Scott and works for the Double J."

"Wha–at?" There was nothing colorless about his eyes now. They flamed with hatred. A choking laugh came from his corded throat. "Of all the — Travis is with the Double J? That lying outfit that drove an honest rancher out of the Flag area?"

Columbine stifled the questions that surfaced instantly in her mind: *Honest? Were you?*

"If it hadn't been for them, we'd be bigger than the Double J and living in a fine house near Flag," he mumbled. Cunning crept into his expression. He turned to go out, then paused. She had the feeling his mind had been far away from the present. "Stick within sight of the ranch house until I say different."

"But that means I can't ride at all," she protested. "You don't expect me to stay cooped up in here, do you?"

"You'll do as I say." His great fist hit the door frame with a solid thud. "And with no backtalk. I won't have another happening like today. There's not a man on the place who wouldn't do the same, including the Cullen whelp. Keep away from all of them." He stomped down the hall.

"I won't," Columbine rebelliously told the walls that had already begun to close in on her. But in the next weeks, she had little choice. Anytime her stepfather rode out, at least one rider remained, conspicuously perched on the corral fence or the porch of the bunkhouse, his face turned in her direction. Being caught by one of Stockton's men offered no better a situation than living in a cage.

The restrictions made their mark. The face in her mirror became paler than ever, the slim figure more finely tuned. Shadows deepened beneath her listless eyes until even Zeke, preoccupied with many thoughts, noticed. "Are you ailing?"

"No, I just miss being able to ride." She toyed with the delicious food she had prepared and laid down her fork. "I don't have much appetite when I can't get out."

The next day, he tapped at the door of her cabin refuge. "The horses are saddled. Come on."

To her amazement, he accompanied her on the first real ride she had taken since he delivered his edict. He even agreed to an impromptu race, and in his heavy-handed manner, complimented her when she beat him back to the corral by several lengths. From then on, they rode almost every afternoon. Yet the knowledge her freedom had been stolen kept Columbine from fully enjoying the exercise. She couldn't help remembering the way Zeke had insulted the dark-haired cowboy from the Double J and burned with shame each time she remembered it. If only she could make up for it!

Her opportunity came unexpectedly and after much prayer. One morning, she stepped outside to the whinny of horses, the chill of impending winter, and an intensely blue sky. Zeke stood frowning on the porch. Andy Cullen lounged in the saddle of a restless horse.

"I suppose you have to go, but get back immediately," Zeke barked.

"Sure, Boss. Soon as I get rid of this dog-goned tooth." Andy touched his scarf-wrapped cheek. He grinned at the girl and raised his voice. "Miss Columbine, you need anything from Flag?"

She started to shake her head but saw the look in Andy's eyes and hesitated. A thrill shot through her. She did need something. Hadn't she been praying about it for days? Scarcely knowing what she replied, she caught Andy's almost imperceptible nod and ran to her room. A list. White thread. A dozen buttons like one she slipped into an envelope. She finished her meager list, dashed off a short note, and without reading it, shoved it into an envelope that folded into the other and tripped lightly down the stairs. "Thanks, A —, er, Cullen." She watched him ride away and forced herself to turn to Zeke. "Breakfast is nearly ready."

Another waiting period began. She mentally rode every foot of the way from the Tonto to Flag and beyond. Andy Cullen rode in just before dusk, cheerful as ever. "Sure glad to get that tooth out, Boss. Here's Miss Columbine's thread and buttons." He handed over a small parcel.

Her spirits sank. Even though she'd tried to tell herself he had no need to answer, her heart protested that Smokey would respond. He hadn't. Never in the world would Andy have entrusted the package to Zeke if it contained anything except her notions. Depressed, she caught the package Zeke tossed and managed to thank Andy. The slight raising of one eyebrow and a quickly hidden grin brightened the evening. Thank God for her one remaining friend on the ranch.

The parcel lay unopened during the hours between its arrival and bedtime. She remembered to take it upstairs with her after bidding Zeke good night. When she shifted it to her left hand so she could open her bedroom door with her right, it crackled. Babbitt's had certainly wrapped it well. Suddenly an idea occurred to her. She stepped inside and felt her way to a table to light a lamp. Taking the precaution of shooting home the sturdy bolt lock Zeke had installed on her door, Columbine ripped open the brown paper. A small sheet of folded white paper fell to the floor. She snatched it up and devoured the contents.

Dear Miss Ames,
    You are always welcome on the Double J, whenever you want to come and for as long as you want to stay. I feel sure that one day you will come. Trust in Andy and in that God of yours and in me.

A tiny campfire with a smudge of smoke served as a signature.

Happy tears crowded behind her eyelids. Much of her despair and loneliness subsided. She read it over, feeling a hidden meaning in the first part. When she came to the last sentence, she halted. *Trust in . . . that God of yours. . . .* Disappointment blotted out her happiness. "God, does this mean he doesn't believe in You? If not, why would he write it this way?" Into the dark morning hours, she wrestled with the knotty problem. Her joy had been tarnished by the revealing words.

Before she could fully interpret the letter, Zeke made a surprising move. One night following their supper meal, he said, "Colley, I've been thinking things over. You're young, and you need a husband. No one can give you what I can. There's trouble brewing. Hadley's coaxed off a bunch of our riders. I won't be able to do the roundup until spring." He leaned forward, and the lamplight showed the rigid way he held his body. "I can wait. The winter and next spring are yours to get ready. Next July, we'll head for Flag and the Fourth of July celebration there. You'll like it. Horse races, a picnic, all kinds of goings-on. Your birthday's the tenth, so we'll stick around Flag and be married then. You'll be eighteen and a woman, just like your mother."

She wanted to hurl the lamp at him, to disclaim any intention of ever taking her mother's place in his life. But an inner warning that to do so meant the loss of even those precious months placed a guard on her lips.

"You hear me, Colley?"

"I do." Lamplight glowed on her lowered head.

Evidently satisfied, Zeke leaned back in his chair. From under downcast lashes, she saw the relaxing of his shoulders. She had promised nothing, but he took it for everything. Did she dare tread on the frail foundation of security formed by his decree? She must. To spend months in the imprisoned state of the past weeks would drive her mad.

"May I ride again? If I take someone, Andy, perhaps? Once the men know what you plan, none of them will dare do anything to challenge you."

"You're not in love with Cullen, are you?"

"No. I never have been, and besides, he has a girl." How good to be able to look him straight in the eye, honestly and without guile. "I thank you for riding with me, but you don't really have the time, do you?"

He hesitated, then grudgingly gave in. "No. As long as Cullen keeps his hands off, it's all right."

"Thank you, Father." She rose, knowing if she didn't leave the room, her triumph would give her away. This small concession meant hope for the future.

"I'll announce it tomorrow."

"All right." What did it matter when or what he proclaimed or to whom? She had taken no vows, given no consent.

The next morning, he called in the re-

178

maining men and said briefly, "I aim to marry Colley on her birthday next July. Until then, Cullen, you'll ride with her when I can't."

For once even Andy appeared speechless. Columbine saw his look of reproach, and she sent him a signal with her eyes. To her relief, he relaxed and said, "Thanks, Boss. I'll take good care of her."

"See that you do, or you'll answer to me." Stockton turned on his heel and strode back into the house.

For the benefit of the outfit, Columbine called, "Bring the horses up at once, Cullen."

"Yes, Ma'am." Stone-faced but with a wink that threatened to send her into hysterics, Andy headed for the bunkhouse, trailed by the others in small chattering groups.

One more bridge remained to be crossed, and Columbine marched toward it waving banners outwardly and cringing on the inside. Fortified by reading her Bible and strengthened by prayer, she approached Zeke. "Will you do something for me, please?"

"Anything." He threw down a paper on which he'd been figuring, a half smile on his lips.

She stood there before him, young, innocent, wearing unconscious pathos. "This is so different and hard for me to get used to. Will you — can you — I just don't want you to kiss me." She brought out her winning hand. "No one's ever kissed me but Mother. Until I'm a bride . . . ?" She clasped her hands.

A dull red suffused his heavy face. Something flickered in his eyes. If she could win this victory, she thought, surely the months that stretched ahead would be bearable.

"All right, Colley." His husky voice betrayed his feelings and won him more respect than he had ever garnered from his stepdaughter.

"Thank you." She held out one slim hand. He took it, clutched it convulsively, then pulled back. She had won another skirmish, one more battle in her fight for freedom. God willing, she would also win the war.

CHAPTER 10

True to his word, Zeke made no demands on Columbine. As late fall slipped into winter, she dreamed only of a dark-eyed cowboy. Twice Andy delivered carefully concealed notes to Smokey; by the same means, she replied.

I hate the secrecy, Smokey wrote to her. *I'd like to ride in and tell Stockton I've come to see you, but Andy says no.*

Her heartbeat quickened when she read the simple words, and she wrote back, warning him not to do anything foolish. Just before Christmas, Andy appeared with horses saddled as usual for their afternoon ride. Snow might blanket the peaks near Flag and fall on the Double J, but winters in the Tonto Basin generally stayed pleasant. So far they had ridden every day. Always Columbine felt Zeke's quick survey of her when she came back, but he said nothing. She made a point of acting natural even when her faithful friend sang the praises of a certain Smokey Travis, causing her to blush profusely.

Once out of earshot of the lounging men on the bunkhouse porch, Andy said in a low voice, "I have a surprise for you."

"Really?" Columbine's mouth turned up. Seldom did they complete a ride without his showing her a late flower, a curious rock formation, or an unusual cloud formation. "Will I like it?"

"I should smile." He did and broke into a contagious laugh.

"Is it big or small?"

"Mmm, medium."

"What color?"

"Lots of colors." He laughed again, and his brown eyes twinkled. "Black and tan, mostly."

"A deer like the one we saw last week?"

He nearly fell from his saddle in his glee. "You might say that. Don't ask so many questions."

"Just one more," she teased. "Is it living or dead?"

His corn-colored hair fell over his forehead from under his sombrero. "Haw, haw! Not dead, that's for sure."

"Then it can't be a rock or a tree," she reasoned aloud. Her comment sent Andy into another spasm. She ignored him and obediently guided her horse after him, too intent on wondering what the surprise might be to pay much attention to the path they took. When Andy reined in his horse, she did the same and looked around. "Why, we're at the cave."

"Wait here," Andy told her mysteriously. He dismounted and tossed his horse's reins over its head. "Think I'll go down to the creek for a drink." Without the usual courtesy of helping her from the saddle, he disappeared over the edge of the hill.

"Well, I never." Columbine indignantly clambered from the saddle. "Andy Cullen, where are your manners?"

"Don't be too hard on him. I asked him to bring you and then leave."

She turned. Smokey Travis leaned against the rock wall of the cave entrance. "Why, how did you, Mr. Travis; you know it's dangerous for you to be here. Why did you come?" She valiantly bit back the glad cry that rose within her.

His white teeth gleamed in his deeply tanned face. "I hankered to see you."

She hated the red tide she felt sweeping her cheeks.

"Are you a little glad to see me?"

"Yes." Her heart pounded when twin

lamps lit up his dark eyes and he took a step toward her.

"Thank you for writing." He gazed down at her. "Could you — would you — call me Smokey? It's my real name," he added.

"Yes, if you would call me Columbine," she murmured, then thought how inane she sounded. She struggled for her usual calm. "Is everything all right — on the ranch where you work, I mean?"

He unsaddled her horse and spread the saddle blanket on a wide, flat-topped rock. Once seated, he regaled her with the adventures of the twins and their new pard, Danny. He went on to tell how Joel once saved his life and shared scenes of the wagon train trek to Flag from Texas. Laughing uncontrollably, he described Curly's courtship, and almost wistfully, he spoke of Joel and Rebecca's wedding. "Wish you'd been there. I never saw Joel or Rebecca look so happy. You'll like her a lot, an' she'll be crazy about you." His admiring look deepened the high color in her face.

"I hope someday I can meet her."

"You will." Something lurked in the cowboy's watching dark eyes and called to her.

She took a deep breath. "I suppose Andy's told you my — my stepfather says I have to marry him on my eighteenth birthday."

"Saying it an' doing it aren't the same," he told her. His brows came together in a frown. "You don't love him, do you?"

She looked down. "No. He's been kind to me, but I don't love him like Mother said a woman must love a man before she marries." She looked up to see his jaw set in a grim line.

"Then keep trusting in that God of yours an' in Andy an' me," he told her quietly.

Impulsively, Columbine laid her slim hand on his. "Smokey, why do you call him my God? He's yours, too." Earnestness turned her blue eyes almost purple. "Don't you believe in Him?"

"Sure. Who could see a grand country like this and not believe?"

His quick reply didn't satisfy her. She gazed unseeingly at the rock cave, the grazing horses, then back at him. "Are you a Christian?" she asked shyly. "Do you believe in Jesus?"

Smokey looked deep into her eyes. "I can't say I'm a Christian, but I believe in Jesus. I've been around Joel an' Gideon an' the others enough to know what He did for even cowpunchers like me." He turned his hand palm up and grasped hers. "It's like this. Once a man signs on a Trailmate like Him, everything's bound to be different.

Then along comes a skunk like Hadley. What's a feller to do? On the one hand, that skunk needs killing. On the other hand, Jesus won't stand for such." Poignancy crept into his expression. "Columbine, do you understand what I'm saying?"

"Yes," she whispered, "but I think you're wrong. I believe when we invite Jesus to ride with us and live in our hearts, He will give us the strength to do what's right, no matter what." She squeezed his hand and realized what she was doing and dropped it.

"If I could believe that, it would make a powerful lot of difference," Smokey muttered.

She wanted deeply to assure him that was true, but a rustling in the woods and the arrival of Andy Cullen forestalled her.

Andy looked apologetic. "Sorry to break up your gab, but if we don't get back to the ranch pretty soon, Zeke will be in a rage."

Smokey stood and helped the girl to her feet. "Before you go, I have something for you." He strode into the cave and came out with a package. "It isn't much, just candy."

"Shall I open it now?"

His face turned crimson. "Why don't you stuff it in your saddle bags an' open it when you get home?" He spun on his heel. "Andy, you're a real pard." The younger man reddened with obvious pleasure.

Slowly Smokey turned back to Columbine. "May I come again?"

"How can you?" she asked, afraid but wanting to say yes. "Won't the Double J think it's strange if you ride off all the time?"

A singularly sweet smile crossed his features. "It won't be all the time. Besides, now that we're carpentering an' getting houses built, there's little night herding. After their last try for our cattle, Hadley an' his gang have been lying low. I put the news out on the range that the rustlers had been recognized, but I didn't give names."

"Smokey, was my stepfather in on that raid?" She held her breath and dug her nails into the palms of her clenched hands.

"No!" Smokey immediately answered. "From what I heard, Hadley talked a bunch of the Z riders into making the raid. Were they ever sore when it didn't amount to anything!"

She sagged in relief. Yet the memory of Zeke saying Hadley had coaxed off part of the outfit and that there would be no roundup this spring played in her mind.

"There's another reason why I might be in these parts," Smokey told them with dead seriousness. "If the Scotts are willing, I'd like to hole up somewhere near here an' just

187

keep an eye on Hadley." *And Stockton,* he wanted to add. His unspoken words hung in the air. Columbine pressed her lips together, torn between the implication and the delight of seeing Smokey again.

He smiled once more. "If I happen to be riding near this spot in, say, two weeks, will you be here?" His glance included Andy, but she knew just how much time that worthy young schemer would spend with them.

"I might." She watched while he resaddled her horse, the years of trail experience evident in his strong hands. Back in the saddle, she leaned down. "Be careful."

"I will." He shrugged. "I reckon a New Mexico cowpuncher can be as clever as one from Arizona." He still stood motionless, arm upraised in farewell, when Andy and Columbine rode away. The next instant, he dropped back weakly to the big rock, bare now of the saddle blanket. "Doggone if she isn't sweeter an' prettier than the first time I saw her." He mopped his hot face with his neckerchief. "She must like me a little, or she wouldn't have half promised to meet me. Her eyes showed she didn't like this sort of sneaking around, but what else can we do?" Deep in thought before heading back to the Double J, Smokey determined to convince Joel and Gideon a spy in the Tonto could be real useful in finding what Hadley and Stockton were planning.

Two weeks later to the day, Smokey rode Buckskin to the well-concealed cave. He peered at the trail but saw no fresh tracks other than the small prints of deer. The thumping of his heart sounded loud enough to scare off a mountain lion. A half hour later, his ears picked up the steady beat of hooves. Earlier, he had made sure Buckskin was off the trail. Chances were slim that a rider would be here other than by appointment, but he'd take no risks.

"Smokey?" Andy's cheerful voice brought him into the open. His heart sank. No slender girl rode beside his friend.

"She's here," Andy assured him. "I just wanted to check first. A time or two lately, I've had the feeling someone's trailing us. It ain't one of our hands, but it could be Hadley."

A little thrill swept through Smokey at the sight of Columbine riding toward him, and he had to admit, at the thought of another confrontation with Hadley. If the rustler meant harm to the girl, trouble lay ahead. He smoothed the frown from his face and stepped forward to help her from her horse, but she had already sprung down. He saw the hesitancy in her face, then a flood of color that gladdened his heart. She *did* like him.

Their strange courtship followed the same general pattern throughout the winter and into the spring. Weather permitting, every two weeks Andy rode with Columbine to the cave. He told Smokey they rode in a different direction each day in case curious eyes took note or plotting men tried to lay in wait. By mid-spring, Stockton had again begun talking of a raid according to Andy, who didn't scorn listening when something interesting was being discussed.

Once, Columbine wandered down to the stream and left the two men alone for a few minutes. Andy whispered, "Hard as it is to believe, I ain't too sure but what Stockton's thrown back in with Hadley."

"Impossible!" Smokey spit out.

"Not permanent-like." Andy tousled his shock of hair. His brown eyes looked worried. "Just for this one big deal. A roundup's likely to include a whole lot more critters than's wearing the Z brand. Shh, here comes Columbine."

Smokey hid his concern and spent the precious time with the one person he had long since realized he wanted for his wife.

190

Reluctantly, at the end of a too-short visit, he watched the two riders out of sight as usual. Once alone, he swung back into the saddle and headed for the Double J, riding all night thanks to a friendly moon that lighted his way. This news had to be passed on.

"Just keep watching and listening," Gideon and Joel ordered.

"What about the girl?" Joel added when he went out with his friend, leaving Gideon behind.

"She's biding her time." Smokey looked deep into the understanding blue eyes. "So am I."

A warm handclasp completed their conversation. After Smokey grabbed a few hours' sleep and packed a supply of grub and clean clothes, he turned south and east. From Flag to the brakes, he had ample time to consider the present and future, to digest what he had learned from Joel, Gideon, and now Columbine.

A slow smile crept over his face. He couldn't help believing she had begun to care. It showed in her honest face, in the little lilt in her voice when she spoke to him, and most of all in the delicate color that tinged her cheeks. An unspoken prayer of thankfulness winged its way from Smokey's troubled heart. The way ahead looked rocky and steep, as tough as any mountain he'd ever had to climb. If only he dared give in to the urge growing stronger every day to turn over the reins to God and His Son. Still he hesitated, every protective bone in his body crying out he must care first for Columbine.

Never had the music of Arizona been sweeter to Columbine Ames's ears than during the spring of 1891. The laughing brook danced and sang its way over amber stones between new-leafed cottonwoods. Each coyote crying for his mate put an echo in her heart. As if for the first time, she watched birds mating and building nests. Would she one day make a home for the dark-eyed cowboy who seemed to have been part of her life forever? The thought always brought a little gasp. She found herself turning to the Bible's great love stories again and again and then to the New Testament verses that likened the love of Christ for His church to that of a bridegroom coming for his bride. Yet at the same time a little voice warned her Smokey had not yet committed his life to the Lord she worshiped and served. Soon she knew he would; he must. Once he realized the only real strength in the world came from God, the next-to-the-last obstacle to their love would be removed.

At this point, inevitably Columbine sighed. How could she and Smokey find happiness as long as Zeke Stockton coveted her? He would fight to the death before he'd let her go. *So would Smokey,* she told herself. *God, if he killed Father, I couldn't bear it. If Father killed him, I wouldn't want to live.* The only time she felt strong enough to endure came while she pored over her Bible and talked with the Lord.

Contrary to range rumors, nothing unusual happened at the Z's spring roundup. Hadley had not been present. Andy reported no more than the usual number of mixed-in brands. To everyone's amazement, Stockton kept a careful tally of those and remarked offhandedly, "I'll see the ranchers are paid for these."

"Maybe he's had a change of heart," Smokey suggested in one of their rare conversations when Columbine wasn't present.

" 'Twouldn't surprise me if he ups and goes straight 'cause of her. Too bad he picked Columbine," Andy said soberly, a little crease between his brows.

Yet Smokey couldn't trust Stockton's apparent turnabout completely. He continued to camp out in the Tonto, wide-eyed and alert, all the time aware of how rapidly spring had rushed into summer. Now June lay over the brakes like a wool blanket, and Columbine's birthday and proposed wedding day loomed closer. So far, he and Andy had come up with no way to rescue her. In desperation, Smokey turned to God.

"You can help," he cried one afternoon to a lightning-filled, thunder-heavy sky. "Isn't there some way to save her without bloodshed?" Only another jagged, crackling bolt and a great clash of thunder replied. He waited. Yet the storm passed, and no still small voice came.

Two days later, Andy and Columbine dashed into the clearing in front of the cave. "Smokey, it's here. Our chance." In all his meetings with her, Smokey had never seen such fire and hope in the usually sad blue eyes. Her words hit him the way lightning strikes tall pines. "Father has to go away on business. He will be gone about two weeks, starting the last day of June."

"That's wonderful, but —"

"Don't you see?" Her breath came in little puffs that stirred the silvery fair hair loose from her hat. *We can't be married on my birthday after all.* Her jewel-like eyes held all the relief Smokey felt in his heart.

"This is the plan," Andy interposed, excitement lighting his face. "Stockton had promised Columbine he'd take her to Flag for the celebration, so ain't it reasonable to say she has permission to go?" He didn't wait for an answer. "The day after he leaves, we'll take her to the Double J. You said she'd be welcome." He grinned. "Once there, if you can't figure out a way to keep her, well . . ." He winked at Smokey. "I'm for a drink from the creek. Why don't you talk things over while I'm gone? It can't be long," he warned. "Zeke's been complaining our rides take too much time."

The moment he disappeared, Smokey lifted Columbine from the saddle. This time, instead of releasing her, he placed a hand on each of her shoulders. "Columbine, I've loved you from the minute I saw you. How would you like to go ahead and be married on your birthday? To me?" His body rigid, he longed to encircle her with his arms and never let her go. "I'd take good care of you, and Zeke or nobody could ever scare you again." He tilted her chin up with one finger and saw a lone tear seep from between downcast lashes. Humility and a sense of awe overtook him as if he stood on the edge of great understanding.

Her lashes swept up, spiky from tears. Her

blue eyes shone tenderly, filled with perfect love and trust. "If you're sure you want me, I'll marry you."

"Sure!" As Smokey's self-control slipped, so did his hands, from her shoulders to her waist. He lowered his head until his lips rested on hers. Her arms tightened. All his wild imaginings hadn't prepared him for the love he discovered at that moment. Instinctively, he knew this was her first kiss; it was his as well.

"Now that's more like it," a laughing voice said from behind them. "I take it there's a wedding coming off? With me as the best man, maybe?"

Smokey freed Columbine just enough so she could lean back, rosy red and smiling. "Not by a long shot! I aim to be the best man at my wedding, but you can stand up with us."

"Andy, we'll never be able to thank you enough." The newly engaged girl faltered. Slipping from Smokey's embrace, she ran to Andy and stood on tip-toe to kiss his lean cheek. A wave of scarlet painted his cheeks as Smokey laughed delightedly.

Andy rubbed his cheek and in his own droll manner retorted, "Say, I can see what they mean about turning the other cheek. This time, it would be a pleasure!" When their laughter died, he reminded, "We have to plan."

Their escape proved so simple that Columbine with all her faith found it surprising, and the two men considered it miraculous. Stockton rode out on schedule. Like many days, the following afternoon, Andy and Columbine mounted for their ride. Their saddlebags, packed in the dead of night, were stuffed to capacity with her clothes and toilette articles. Columbine wore the same outfit for riding she always wore to allay possible suspicion.

Unlike the other days, they did not plan to come back, ever. Before Zeke returned, Columbine would be Mrs. Smokey Travis, and Andy, a valuable part of the Double J.

CHAPTER 11

"Snappin' crocodiles, but yu've gone and done it!" Open admiration for both Columbine's loveliness and his pard's close-mouthed courtship shone in Jim Perkins's face.

"This is Columbine Ames," announced Smokey simply at the Double J dinner gathering. "Her stepfather is Zeke Stockton, an' she's running away from him. You're all invited to our wedding on July tenth; she'll be eighteen then."

The chorus of welcomes and warm embraces by the women threatened to undermine Columbine's resolve. Silently, she appealed to Smokey with a fleeting look and five minutes later found herself in a tastefully decorated room.

"Your home until the wedding," Judith Scott told her. "You have nothing to be frightened about." Her eyes filled. "I know what it's like to be alone and uncertain."

Another quick hug and she vanished, leaving Columbine to kneel by the spotless counterpane on the inviting bed and pour out her gratitude to God.

Merry-eyed Rebecca Fairfax Scott solved a problem when she drew the newcomer aside. "I'd be proud if you'd wear my wedding dress," she offered hesitantly, her brown eyes shining. "I'm just a few inches taller, and we can take it up and in."

"You're so kind." Still bewildered by the openhearted way the entire Double J had taken her in, she fought tears. "I-I didn't know what to do. I don't have anything suitable with me and somehow . . ." Her voice trailed off.

"You'd rather not be married in something bought with Stockton's or Smokey's money," Rebecca finished for her. "That's what I figured. Now, come see my new home and we'll work on the dress."

So much to see, so much to do! Columbine discovered she didn't have much time alone with Smokey. In a way, she felt glad. The days between her arrival at the ranch and her birthday provided a little breathing space. Soon the white gown hung ready and waiting. The cabin Smokey had shared with Curly received a thorough scrubbing and would house the newlyweds as it had Curly and his wife until their own cabin could be completed. Columbine drifted through the hours wondering if Smokey were thinking of her, of the wedding, *of their future.* Every sight of the dark-eyed cowboy sent a thrill to her heart.

The object of her adoration could barely do the work assigned him for dreaming of his loved one. A dozen times a day he shook himself back to the present from joyful anticipation. Not until Jim Perkins goaded Joel into entering Querida in the annual Fourth of July race did Smokey fire up. "Boss, we've all been hankering for a real showdown between your Kay-reeda an' Rebecca's Vermilion. How about it?"

Joel's blue eyes glistened with boyish fun, then a more mature look came. "Rebecca can't ride him." He flushed bright red, and a delighted grin swept over his face. "There's going to be a little Joel or Becky."

"That's good news, but you can't get out of it so easy. I caught an' broke that red mustang stallion," Smokey reminded. "Besides, it's more fair this way. We're nearer of a weight an' the horses can start even."

The result of the conversation showed up when Flag and half the country reached town the morning of the Fourth. Smokey proudly rode to the starting line. Vermilion glistened in the sun, polished and prancing. His faithful friend Querida's black coat shone as if she'd been oiled. A sigh rippled through the half-dozen riders mounted on the finest horses they could muster, and Smokey's eyes gleamed. He said in an undertone, "Mighty fine nags, but they'll never catch Vermilion. Neither will Kay-reeda."

Joel's teeth flashed white, and his spontaneous laugh turned heads. "Only because she's going to be in front of him. *Way* in front!"

Smokey snorted but contented himself with an answering grin and the knowledge no horse alive could outrun the red stallion, given the same start. He let Vermilion dance a bit more but not enough to take the edge off, then crouched in the saddle, body bent forward. Joel did the same.

Crack! The starting pistol fired. The line of horses leaped ahead. "Yippee-ay!" Andy called. Smokey barely heard him. With his gaze fixed directly between Vermilion's ears, he knew Querida ran beside them, nose even with the stallion's flank. By the end of the first quarter mile, six valiant riders struggled to catch the pair far in the lead. Smokey urged Vermilion into the flowing dead run that ate up the ground. Querida stuck like a leech. At the end of the next quarter mile, they stayed the same. Then with a wild cowboy yell, Joel goaded Querida into a spurt of speed that brought the black mare and her rider slightly ahead of the red.

Vermilion snorted. Smokey knew he didn't like the reversed position. He leaned forward and called in the stallion's ear. Vermilion increased his pace. At the end of the third quarter mile, he ran neck and neck with Querida.

Three hundred yards to go. Two hundred. A hundred. Smokey could hear the deafening roar of the excited crowd. He flattened himself until he almost lay on Vermilion's neck. From the corner of his eye, he could see Joel do the same.

Fifty yards. Thirty. Twenty. Ten. Across the finish line they swept! Had he won? Smokey couldn't tell. He let Vermilion run on and gradually slackened the reins, aware of Querida beside him. Men and beasts came to a stop some distance from the yelling crowd. Smokey shoved back his sombrero and wiped the sweat from his forehead. "Who won?"

"I'm hanged if I know!" Joel burst into laughter. "Shall we go see?"

To the delight of the crowd, they rode

back together. Jim Perkins's bellow sounded above the screams. "Snappin' crocodiles, if that ain't the purtiest tie I ever saw!"

"Tie?" Smokey gasped.

"We tied?" Joel doubled over and laughed until tears came. "Put her there, Pard." He gripped Smokey's hand.

"Here's to a couple of grand horses," Smokey told him before bursting at the seams. "Haw haw! If Vermilion and Kay-reeda didn't put one over on us, then I'm a lop-eared mule." He glanced both ways to make sure no one could hear. "At that, I'm glad."

"So am I." Joel wiped his eyes. "If my horse had beaten Rebecca's, she'd never have let me hear the last of it, and vice versa." They walked their steaming mounts to nearby shade and rubbed them down, then rejoined the rest of the Double J for the usual Fourth of July fun.

Columbine's eyes rounded at sights new and strange. Smokey glowed with pride and didn't miss a single envious glance or the way the young bucks "dropped by" to greet him and meet his sweetheart. Good-naturedly, he told them, "Go find your own gals. This one's spoken for by me."

Smokey entered both pistol and rifle contests, outdone by Gideon and Joel in the pistol match but winning first place in the rifle shoot. Andy Cullen came close and took second. His big grin showed how good he felt about being on and a part of the Double J. Jim Perkins loftily informed his friends Conchita had begged him not to enter and show them up. "Anything for a lady," he smirked. When Smokey challenged him to an informal shooting match, he raised an eyebrow, snatched his Colt revolver from its holster, and blazed away at a discarded target with every shot hitting the bull's-eye. Smokey threw up his hands and refused to follow what he called a lucky shooting spree.

As the early days of July crawled by, there was only one bitter drop in the honey of Smokey and Columbine's love: Smokey's indecision to accept Jesus Christ. If he did, he knew he couldn't live up to it, especially if Stockton came calling. Columbine's blue eyes showed how desperately she longed for his commitment, but she said little.

The night before their wedding, he left her and rode out onto the range, the place where he did his best thinking. The midnight blue velvet sky spangled with stars, the pungent smell of sage crushed by Buckskin's hooves, and the whispering aspen leaves left a bittersweet feeling in his heart.

"The one thing she's ever wanted I can't give her," he told the night sky. Buckskin pricked up her ears and slowed her pace. "God, I know it isn't enough if I do it for her. It has to be for me an' You an' because I know it's right." He sighed and shoved his sombrero back on his dark hair. "All those months ago, what Joel said about the voice. Well, I've felt Arizona wind an' the earth shake from thunder an' seen lightning set fires. Why haven't I heard that still small voice?" Restlessness filled him. The void he'd managed partly to fill with love and dreaming yawned deeper and lonelier than ever. "God, where *is* that voice, anyway?"

Only the crooning of the wind and rustling of leaves answered him. He remained silent, slumped in the saddle, filled with the wonder of night. A long time later, Columbine's face flashed into his mind. He recalled her voice and the look in her eyes when she whispered, *I believe when we invite Jesus to ride with us and live in our hearts, He will give us the strength to do what's right, no matter what.* The wind ceased. The rustling halted. But the whispered memory sang on . . . *invite Jesus . . . strength to do right . . . no matter what.*

On the verge of the most important discovery in his life, Smokey felt blinders being lifted from his eyes. "After the fire," he breathed. Hadn't Columbine passed through the fires of fear and trouble? Their refining process had made her what she was, a witness for her Lord. "God, is the still small voice *You* speaking through *her?*" His heart felt like it might burst. "The same as when You talked to folks in the Bible an' how I feel when Joel an' Gideon preach Your Word?"

Buckskin stopped, and Smokey looked down. Moonlight shone on the fork in the trail. One way led to the ranch, the other to Flag. "Old gal, it's time we — both of us — headed for home." He bowed his head. "The reins are Yours, no matter what." No longer need he search to hear a mysterious voice.

On her wedding morning, Columbine received a gift from her soon-to-be husband: a note scrawled in bold handwriting as black as his hair and eyes. Through wet eyes, she read: NOW HE'S MY TRAILMATE, TOO.

At ten o'clock on her eighteenth birthday, Columbine Ames, a vision in white, became Smokey Travis's wife. The cowboy's open declaration of faith, announced publicly just before the ceremony, left no dry eyes on the Double J. "I asked Jesus to ride with me from now on," he stated. His gaze rested on Jim Perkins, Joel, Curly, and Andy. "I've had a lot of good pards, but He is different. From now on, I'll be heading where He leads me, I mean, us." He smiled at Columbine, whose soft hand lay on his arm. His confession provided the sweetest background music for the marriage vows.

At twelve o'clock, Smokey's newfound faith suffered its first attack: Zeke Stockton rode in. His colorless eyes aflame, he leaped from the saddle before his horse skidded to a stop.

"Where is she?" he roared at Andy Cullen, who lounged on the front porch. "You dirty pup, I ought to kill you."

Andy paled but stood his ground and said nothing.

"What are you, dumb? *Where's my daughter?*"

The commotion brought folks running. They swarmed to the porch, up from the corral and the bunkhouse, until a crowd surrounded the livid intruder.

"I'm here, Father." Columbine, pale as the frail flower whose name she bore, slowly crossed the porch, still gowned in white.

"What the — Colley, what are you doing here dressed like that?" Zeke reeled and rubbed his eyes. "A wedding dress? But you didn't know I could get here in time! Why did you leave the ranch?"

She blanched until her blue eyes shone bright against her face. "I —" She swayed and would have fallen if Smokey hadn't sprung forward to support her.

"You!" Stockton hissed. A hint of foam came to his lips, and his big frame quivered.

"She's my wife, Stockton." Smokey's voice rang loud in the quiet assembly.

"No, no!" The rancher clawed for his gun, but his fingers stilled when Smokey called, "I'm not armed."

"Get a gun, or so help me, I'll kill you where you stand," Stockton yelled. Columbine gave a piteous cry. He ignored her. "Travis, get a gun if you don't want to be shot."

The moment Smokey dreaded and had known he must face was here. *God, help me,* he prayed silently.

"Coward! Skunk!" Zeke fired off every range epithet, his face black with rage, fingers twitching. "Are you a man or a sneaking yellow dog?" He strode toward Smokey, who had come down the steps to face him. "For the last time, will you get a gun?"

The strength to do right, no matter what. Indecision fled. Smokey looked straight into

Zeke's eyes. "No."

Disbelief rushed into Zeke's face. His mouth dropped. "You'll stand here and take what no man should and not fight back?" An ugly laugh rolled out. "You, who rode in calm as a summer day, knowing what Hadley had told me? I'd never have figured you for a yellow-belly!"

Smokey said nothing.

Stockton's contemptuous glance swept the crowd. Smokey followed his look. Not an armed man there except Zeke. A thin smile crossed the haggard face. Zeke deliberately drew his Colt and aimed it directly at Smokey's heart. He cocked the gun. "I reckon a dead husband won't stand in the way for me to marry Colley," he taunted.

Smokey didn't move a muscle.

"Why, Travis? Is it 'cause I'm her daddy?"

Smokey squared his shoulders, and a smile creased his face. "No, Stockton. Yesterday I'd have shot you an' felt bad for Columbine. Now I won't. I turned my life over to God last night an' He don't hold with killing, no matter what." He heard a gasp and a rush of flying feet as Columbine swept down the steps to him. She planted herself between him and Zeke. For the first time, Smokey felt fear. The red rage in Stockton's eyes showed he had gone beyond

209

reason. "Columbine, get back!" He grabbed her white-clad arm and tried to swing her out of harm's way.

"No." Her voice rang out like a silver bell. "Father, I love him. The same way you loved Mother and she loved you."

Once Smokey had seen a swooping eagle brought down by a bullet. Columbine's voice had the same effect on her stepfather. He flinched, then staggered. The revolver shook in one trembling hand. "You wouldn't want to live without him?" Deadly earnestness drove every word into Smokey's brain.

Columbine cried out, "I would go on living but in the same way you have since Mother died!"

Pain contorted Zeke's face. The Colt fell from his fingers as he stared at the girl, his face the color of long-dead ashes. An eternity later, he said heavily, "I reckon that won't be necessary." He looked deep into her blue eyes and then at Smokey, who knew his face showed compassion and understanding. The cowboy realized the struggle in the older man's soul between memory of the sweet mother whose love he had hoped to regain through her daughter and the desire to spare Columbine the agony he carried.

Like an aged man, he walked to his horse

and climbed into the saddle. He turned to Smokey. "If I ever hear you've mistreated her in any way, I'll kill you, Travis. Armed or not, it won't make any difference." He spurred his horse and rode off before Smokey could reply.

Columbine's high-pitched cry followed him, "Good-bye, Father. God bless you!"

Like animals frozen in a blizzard, the figures in the yard of the Double J watched him ride away, a man beaten by a stripling cowboy with a mighty God. Horse and rider swept around a bend, and Smokey swallowed hard. In years to come, Stockton might look back and curse himself for not killing Smokey and abducting Columbine. Now, however, he had risen to the challenge between good and evil. Smokey turned to his bride, gently picked her up, and carried her away from the sordid scene to the sweet-smelling cabin changed to a bower by loving hands. Once inside, he was about to close the door when Jim Perkins's voice reached them. "Snappin' crocodiles, I never saw anythin' like that before!"

Two weeks later, news of a terrible fight among outlaw bands in the Tonto reached the Double J. At first no one seemed to know who or how many had been killed, but ranchers speculated there'd be a lot fewer missing cattle in the future. Smokey hated to tell Columbine. Despite the great joy their marriage had brought, a shadow lingered in her cameo face and sweet blue eyes.

"There's been trouble," he finally said. "We don't know what men were killed, but Andy and I are riding to the Z to find out."

Every trace of color fled. "Don't go! Smokey, I can't bear it if anything happens to you, too."

"Whoa, we don't know anything's happened to Zeke," he protested, not really believing his words but unwilling for her to worry.

"How long will you be gone?"

"No longer than it takes to — to do what we have to."

Quick understanding filled her eyes.

"Will you stay with Judith or Rebecca?" Smokey wanted to know.

Columbine shook her head. "No. I'll stay here in our own home." She kissed him good-bye and waved from the porch, just as he had pictured her doing all those times in the past when he daydreamed about her. Smokey rode out with Andy, silent and filled with dread. What would they find in the wild, untamed heart of Arizona?

"It can't be much worse," Andy said

soberly when they got to the Z. Corrals stood empty. So did the bunkhouse. The door of the ranch house sagged partway open, and when they stepped inside, dust lay thick on the furniture.

The sight of a forgotten apron on the back of a chair made Smokey draw in a deep breath. *Thank God Columbine had escaped before all of this,* he thought suddenly.

A slight sound from overhead sent the riders hurrying up the stairs. Faint moans guided them to a large room. Zeke Stockton, naked to the waist, his eyes dull with fever, was lying in a clutter of crumpled bedclothes. His head and chest were wrapped with blood-stained bandages. As the two men crossed the room, he showed no surprise. He knew who they were.

"Man, you need a doctor." Smokey attacked the bedding. "Andy, heat water. I'll do what I can."

"Too late." Zeke shook his matted, bandaged head. His cough brought blood to his lips. "I'm done for. No," he added when Smokey opened his mouth to protest, "it's all right." He coughed again, harder this time, an effort that seemed to sap his remaining strength. "Tell Colley I was all wrong. Got her and her mother mixed up. Tell her Hadley's dead; the others ran off the rest of my stock. Doesn't matter now."

Smokey caught Andy's pitying look that clearly asked if Zeke's mumble came from fever.

"Her mother used to pray for me. So did Colley. I knew I should listen. Too late to change a lot of things."

"It's never too late to tell God you're sorry." Smokey spoke loudly in an effort to penetrate Zeke's fading consciousness. "Zeke, Jesus died for all of us so our sins could be forgiven." His voice sounded clear and sure in the quiet room.

"Tell Colley to sell the place. Pay back the ranchers I stole from."

Andy's mouth dropped open.

"I'll tell her," Smokey promised. He could see the struggle Stockton was making to get things off his mind. His heart leaped.

"Tell Colley . . ." Zeke's eyes closed with weariness. The next minute, he opened them and stared at Smokey with a look of wonder, then closed them again. A final breath came and with it a look of peace never before seen on the rancher's face.

Smokey and Andy buried him next to his wife. After locking up the sprawling ranch house, they rode away together. For a long time, neither spoke, then Andy said in a gruff voice, "What are you going to tell

Columbine?"

"The truth."

"Which is — what? I ain't too sure. There at last, seemed like he did what he could do to make things right."

"Only God knows Zeke Stockton's heart at the moment," Smokey reminded.

He repeated the words to a weeping Columbine after they reached the Double J. He had asked Andy to be present when he broke the news.

"He frightened me, but until Mother died, he was kind," Columbine remembered out loud when they had faithfully given her his messages.

"He died with a peaceful look on his face," Andy put in. For once his hair lay flat without brushing; his brown eyes held no laughter. "I kinda think he really was sorry, maybe even told God so when he couldn't get it out."

"We will never know." Smokey placed his arm around his wife's shoulders. "We do know God forgives even the worst sin. All we can do is hope and leave Zeke with Him."

Columbine nodded, and Andy shuffled off. That evening, she and Smokey walked to a promontory not far from their cabin. From it, they could see the intersecting trails, all leading in different directions. "Like our lives," she observed sagely.

"Yes. It's been a long, hard trail here." Smokey held her close, her fair head on his strong shoulder. "Only God knows what's ahead."

A calf bawled in the distance, followed by the distant sounds of a night herding. The western sky blushed, bathing them in rose and gold and purple shadows. Then as the music of the mountains stilled into the hush of twilight, Smokey and Columbine turned their steps toward home.

Dear Readers,

I hope you enjoyed reading *Music in the Mountains*, the third title in the Frontier Brides collection series, as much as I enjoyed writing it. My parents had a deep love for reading and western history. They passed it on to my brothers and me. One Christmas during hard times Mom splurged and bought Dad twenty Zane Grey books. (The $14. gift provided many happy hours reading by kerosene lamp light.)

After World War 2 ended and money wasn't so tight, we camped all over the western states and saw places we already knew from Zane Grey's accurate descriptions. Those trips strengthened my desire to write western novels "someday."

"Someday" came years later when in 1977 I felt called to walk off my government job and write full-time. Now, with six million copies of my 140+ "Books You Can Trust" sold, I marvel. God chose an ordinary logger's daughter to help make the world a better place by providing inspirational reading.

May the Frontier Brides series bring a smile, a tear, inspiration, and hope to each of you.

In His Service,
Colleen L. Reece

The employees of Thorndike Press hope you have enjoyed this Large Print book. All our Thorndike, Wheeler, and Kennebec Large Print titles are designed for easy reading, and all our books are made to last. Other Thorndike Press Large Print books are available at your library, through selected bookstores, or directly from us.

For information about titles, please call:
  (800) 223-1244

or visit our Web site at:
  http://gale.cengage.com/thorndike

To share your comments, please write:
  Publisher
  Thorndike Press
  10 Water St., Suite 310
  Waterville, ME 04901